FREEDOM FABLES

FREEDOM FABLES

SATIRES AND POLITICAL WRITINGS

ROKEYA SAKHAWAT HOSSAIN

TRANSLATED FROM THE
ORIGINAL BENGALI BY KALYANI DUTTA

zubaan

ZUBAAN
128B Shahpur Jat, 1st floor
NEW DELHI 110 049
Email: contact@zubaanbooks.com
Website: www.zubaanbooks.com

First published by Zubaan Publishers Pvt. Ltd 2019

ISBN 978 93 85932 48 9

Zubaan is an independent feminist publishing house based in New Delhi with a strong academic and general list. It was set up as an imprint of India's first feminist publishing house, Kali for Women, and carries forward Kali's tradition of publishing world-quality books to high editorial and production standards. *Zubaan* means tongue, voice, language, speech in Hindustani. Zubaan publishes in the areas of the humanities, social sciences, as well as in fiction, general non-fiction, and books for children and young adults under its Young Zubaan imprint.

Typeset in Bell MT by Jojy Philip, New Delhi 110 015
Printed and bound at Thomson Press India Ltd.

for

the late Dr Parthasarathy Gupta
eminent historian and generous friend,
whose long loan of *Rokeya Rachanabali*
made this book possible

CONTENTS

ACKNOWLEDGEMENTS

Thanks are due to many friends who fuelled my enthusiasm for Rokeya Sakhawat Hossain's writing. The late Dr Parthasarathy Gupta, who generously shared his copy of *Rokeya Rachanabali* with me, a volume which is now difficult to acquire. Friends Narayini Gupta and Debjani Sengupta, who stimulated my tardy project of translating Rokeya's works by bringing me books related to the writer from Dhaka and Kolkata.

Urvashi Butalia of Zubaan, known to me since her pioneering days as a publisher, agreed to be associated with the project after reading just one of the fables, with only one tentative enquiry as to what I intended to do with the two short satires. She concurred with my decision to supplement the two fables with six other pieces by Rokeya, where the writer spiritedly responds and reacts to the events of those early and heady days of the Independence movement. Meghna Singh, my editor, deserves to be thanked profusely for supplying correctives.

While various members of the family were uniformly encouraging, special thanks are due to my son Arindam for being a critical reader who ruthlessly censured instances of imprecise language.

With the kindness and help of all these friends, the frail vessel of *Freedom Fables* now sails forth.

Kalyani Dutta

November 2018

INTRODUCTION

In *Narimoner Aloy*, published in 1989,[1] Arati Gangopadhay raises a question in the context of the extensive economic and political changes seen in Bengal over the last two hundred years: 'Did all this leave no mark upon the minds of our women?' As literature is both the source and subject of sociological analysis, male authors are invariably studied, according to Gangopadhay, for this kind of enquiry in preference over women writers, who have been perceived as emotional and rationally deficient.

In the spirit of the question raised by Gangopadhay, *Freedom Fables* brings together two satires and a collection of articles written by Rokeya Sakhawat Hossain between 1905 and 1932, which assess this alert, combative writer's response to political events and trends seen during three of the most turbulent decades in the history of pre-Independence India. The phrase 'political writings' in this volume's subtitle does not signify exposition of any political theory or ideals on Rokeya's part. Nor are there rebuttals of politicians' statements on behalf of a political party. Rather than working within the male-dominated sphere of politics and governance, Rokeya was absorbed in the work of establishing a school for girls of orthodox Muslim families over the opposition of the community—part of her larger aim to liberate women from circumstances oppressing their lives and minds.

In those early years of the twentieth century, there was nationwide upheaval and new directions in the modern phase of the Indian Independence movement. These stirrings in the city of Calcutta and the nation engaged Rokeya's lively mind. Believing that 'We [women] are one half of the nation. If we fall behind, how will society progress?',[2] she responded to events and utterances affecting the struggle against colonial rule in frequent, incisive articles. The ebb and flow in the fortunes of the Congress party, the Satyagraha Movement, the Swadeshi Andolan, communal rivalries, revolutionaries, famines—all of these drew, from her, interested observations, sometimes laced with scathing humour. She was not unaware of developments in the world outside India, and especially alert if two of her primary interests were involved i.e. resistance to European expansionism and women's emancipation. In 'Rasana Puja' (Pleasing the palate[3]) she referred to the victory of tiny Japan, an Asian nation, over powerful Russia during the Russo-Japanese war. She wished to share with her readers her excitement over the modern reforms introduced in Afghanistan by Sultan Amanullah Khan and his queen, especially those concerning education for girls, and she deplored that they had been rejected by the Afghan people. For this purpose, she translated an Urdu article by a Mumbai teacher, 'Interview with Begum Tarzi', into Bengali.[4] Similar inclinations brought forth a laudatory reference to the social reforms effected in Turkey and Egypt in her address to the Bengal Women's Education Conference in 1926.[5]

It is important to note one unique, invariable feature of all of Rokeya's interventions in political discourse: an unwavering gaze upon how women and their agency are implicated within each issue. In this respect, a statement made by Ellen Brinks in her chapter on Pandita Ramabai[6] deserves attention: 'Both Indian Christians and Hindu feminists had to compete with a nationalism that was rendering the social reforms directed at women secondary to the political goal of Independence.'[7] That relegation of women to the periphery is precisely what Rokeya resisted. For her, the two freedoms—the nation's and that of its women—were equally essential and required unremitting struggle.

There seems to be no need to establish her as a fighter for women's rights and liberty. As early as 1905, in her brilliant utopian fantasy 'Sultana's Dream', with instinctive understanding she displayed every nuance of feminist politics. Resentment at the oppressive control patriarchy asserts under the cloak of religion brought forth a furious attack from Rokeya in 'Amader Abanati' (Our degradation[8]):

> We have fallen as low as it is possible. Yet we have never raised our heads against this subjugation. The most important reason is that whenever a sister has tried to raise her head, the pretext of religion or commands from holy books have been used as weapons to smash her head.
>
> To keep us in darkness, men have declared

religious texts as commands from God... So, you see, these religious texts are nothing but manmade rules and regulations.

So explosive was the reaction to these comments made by Rokeya in that early article that five passages, including the lines quoted above here, that they were subsequently excised by the publisher of the first volume of *Motichur* and perhaps with Rokeya's permission it was renamed and published as 'Stri Jatir Abanati' (Degradation of women) in 1905.

In this context, it is surprising that scholars writing on Indian women living at the cusp of the late nineteenth to early twentieth century seem to be oblivious of Rokeya's work. Shahida Lateef's important book *Muslim Women in India: Political and Private Realities 1890s–1980s*,[9] published in 1990, discusses the contributions of many prominent Muslim women of the time. However, in the chapter 'Growth of the Indian Women's Movement and the Attack on Purdah',[10] Rokeya is absent from Lateef's scrutiny, even though Rokeya's tragi-comic account of the impact of purdah on women, 'Abarodh Basini', had been available in Roushan Jahan's English translation since 1981.[11] The movement for women's enfranchisement, as described by Lateef, was a united action undertaken by Indian women led by Sarojini Naidu. However, though Lateef might not mention it, Naidu was aware of Rokeya's active interest in issues concerning women's rights and enlisted her help.

Not owing affiliation to any political party, Rokeya did not usually indulge in active politics. Yet, when her interest and energy were aroused, she dealt with her responsibilities efficiently. The Anjuman-i-Khawatin-i-Islam, an organisation of Muslim women created with the intention of discussing their issues amongst themselves, was being formed in several important Indian cities, promoted under the leadership of prominent women from Aligarh, Hyderabad, Lahore, and Calcutta. Rokeya established the Calcutta branch in 1916. In 1919 an all-India convention of the Anjuman was held in Calcutta. Rokeya organised the venue and other arrangements. During the Calcutta Congress presided over by Annie Besant, Rokeya assembled a corps of women volunteers. Her addresses at the conferences over which she presided or which she had attended had been much admired, especially in Calcutta (1926) and Aligarh (1925 and 1932).

Yet even writers concentrating on Bengali women of the period, such as Chitra Ghosh, in *Women Movement Politics in Bengal*,[12] are completely unaware of Rokeya's activism. One has to surmise that, due to her being dismissed as only the founder of a girl's school, Rokeya's considerable literary output was ignored. The writings of Pandita Ramabai, the earlier firebrand, were well-known in the West, since she wrote in English. Rokeya was not known outside the confines of Bengali Muslim journals. She had little to no impact on canonical Bengali authors. In the introduction to '*Nari o Poribar: Bamabodhini Potrika*', Bharati Ray noted that in this well-known journal, established by Brahmo men for women's writing, contributions by Muslim women, including Rokeya, were absent.[13]

Given that Rokeya's agenda was to convince society to release the stranglehold upon women's minds and lives, hard-hitting communication rather than literary fame was in her sights. She wrote prolifically and the Calcutta journals of the time afforded a welcome forum for her ideas. Urdu was the medium of instruction in her school, but she preferred to write in Bengali, since home-dwelling, secluded women were her constituency.

Rokeya was a polemicist; she would twist and turn a topic till she reached the conclusion she desired. She made clever use of rhetorical devices. Satire, irony, fables, dream visions, parodies were all in her arsenal as a social commentator. According to Sonia Nishat Amin, Rokeya chose to write in a form, satire, 'that bhadra-mahila were not disposed to favour.'[14]

Four selections in *Freedom Fables* fall into this category. Dream visions, such as the popular 'Sultana's Dream', were a favourite of Rokeya's, a form affording scope for daring innovations. In this collection, 'Shristi Totwo' ('The Essence of Creation') from 1920 belongs to that genre. The two fables, for which this book is named, are both satires and allegories: 'Gyanphal' is designated as a 'rup-rekha', or an allegory, by the author. 'Muktiphal' she called a 'rup-katha', a fairy tale. A barb of irony is hidden here, I feel. To call a story about the very real suffering of Indians under colonialism a 'fairy tale'—a story about the very real famine, hunger, poverty and the wily manipulations of rulers—appears to be a kind of intentional mockery. These two fables were first written and published in 1907, when the split in the Indian National Congress occurred, instigating Rokeya to write 'Muktiphal'. In 1921, these stories were collected and published in the second edition of *Motichur*. It is the versions published in *Motichur* that have been translated for this volume.

These two short satires are at the core of *Freedom Fables*. 'Gyanphal' ('The Tree of Knowledge') and 'Muktiphal' ('The Freedom Tree') were written with Rokeya's characteristic witty humour, which had made her 'Sultana's Dream' so universally popular. As far as the allegories are concerned, one must appreciate the adroitness in presenting the twists and turns of India's two-hundred-year relationship with the imperial British, all within the space of two quite short stories.

'Gyanphal', compact in form and size though temporally vast in scope, begins with the Garden of Eden and swiftly arrives at an idealised Bharat, to depict how a trading company beguiles prosperous Kanakadwipa and succeeds in its ruination.

'Muktiphal', almost a sequel, less gnomic, zeroes in upon the rise and growth of the Indian Congress party as it devised ways of emancipating the country. Rokeya wrote this story after the split in the Congress party into moderates and extremists in 1907.

For this story, Rokeya telescoped, in all of seven episodes, the twenty-two years from the founding of the Congress party in 1885 to 1907, when it split into two factions at Surat. The split must have then seemed to her as the end of the road, as far as offering a strong opposition to the alien power was concerned. In other parts of India too the same kind of dismay and distress was felt. In Maharashtra, K P Khadilkar, a popular playwright, wrote *Kichak Vadha (Death of Kichak)* on this occasion. He allegorised an episode of the Mahabharata wherein Yudhishthira represented Gokhale, the leader of the moderates; the usurper General Kichak was Lord Curzon; Bhima was identified with the extremists; and Draupadi became India. Interestingly, both Rokeya and Khadilkar chose figurative forms for presenting this political crisis and two dethroned queens as victims.[15]

At the time of its reprinting in 1921, in the journal *Motichur II*, Rokeya cautioned that she had made a few extensions to 'Muktiphal'. The fourteen years from 1907 till 1921 saw a dispirited Congress rejuvenate itself, touched by Gandhi's magic. One could surmise that the emergence of Gandhi and the mass mobilisation of people, especially of women, may have inspired her to make changes. The other reason could have been the spread of revolutionary groups in the '20s. Those years are captured by Rokeya in the last few pages of the seventh episode, in 'Muktiphal'.

It should be noted that the strict linearity in the narration of the vast timescape traversed by the two stories would have weighed the stories down; however, Rokeya allows fiction a free run. The fabulous floats easily over mere facts, intriguing the reader with suggestiveness; real personalities, situations, attitudes lurk just beyond view. These are stories where Adam and Eve, the Almighty himself, djinns, paris, demons, Mayavi magicians and the charmed flautist Mayadhar play decisive roles.

In 'Gyanphal', there is constant reference to the exchange of various fruits and rice. 'Muktiphal' revolves around the theme of reviving the mother by feeding her the centennially blooming freedom fruit. Food was important in a fable about a country where the population was decimated repeatedly due to crop failure and administrative mismanagement.

The personae, in these stories, can be as exalted as Hava from the Bible and as fallen as Kangalini, the usurped, emaciated Queen of Bholapur, a country of simpletons. Kangalini, an unidealised Bharatmata, has six sons who represent types of Indian politicians active at that time, as well as their opponents. Her daughters Sumati and Shrimati are both intelligent and courageous like the women of 'Sultana's Dream.'

'Gyanphal', sweeping and upbeat, presents India as Kanakadwipa, a land of gold. The chaotic state into which the Congress and its internal squabbles had led the country and the freedom movement induced in the mind of the writer of 'Muktiphal' a mood of sardonic humour. The Bholapur story is more populous, with Kangalini's children, Mayapur's courtiers, ogres and magicians all scurrying between different locations: earthly hut, forested foothills and a royal court.

Although very little of the continuously shifting reality of the contemporary political situation escaped Rokeya's attention, in 'Muktiphal', she does not allow the fictive world she constructs to be breached with recognisable names. The symbolic names of the actors fix them as types of Indian politicians active on the national stage at the time. She shows witty inventiveness in nativising the word 'boycott', a successful Swadeshi strategy, into 'bykata'. The way the leaders of the Congress party squandered away the impetus of unitedly opposing and cornering the colonial government dismayed her. 'Political caricature' was how a contemporary reviewer in the *Bongiyo Musalman Sahityo Potrika* saw it. The 'moderate faction' of the Congress Party is the focus of much of the comedy and ridicule. Also worth appreciating is the way in which Rokeya catches inflections of supercilious pride and patronage, distilled from the words and proclamations of many colonial officials, in the interactions of the djinn rulers and Mayapuri court officials in sections two and five of 'Muktiphal'.

These two fables enforce Rokeya's conviction that any civilisation that defrauds its women, the natural inheritors of knowledge and wisdom, is bound to collapse. Both stories end with an idealised vision where, in both Kanakadwipa and in Bholapur, the men and women strive together to resuscitate the nation. For Rokeya in 1907, so distant from 1947, there could have been no other conclusion possible.

In order to serve her purposes as a writer and to seize the attention of her women readers, Rokeya devised an idiosyncratic style of her own. It is an informal style, interspersed with snippets of poetry, sometimes her own short poems or a few lines from Tagore or a country saying. However, caught up as she was in the full flow of her writing, Rokeya often does not mention the name of the person she is quoting—tracing her references then becomes a near-impossible task for her contemporary readers, as demonstrated by a few translations included in this volume. Nonetheless, her seamless incorporation of Urdu sentences and English quotations gives the impression of a mind brimming with ideas, opinions. Rokeya and Ismat Chughtai share this quality of colloquial wit, which imparts a tart flavour to their language and takes readers into their confidence.

Rokeya also makes interesting use of emotional appeals along with rational arguments, as found in a short piece 'Subah Sadek' ('True Dawn') from 1931. The author's footnotes often serve as asides in a conversation, for instance in 'Shristi Totwo', where on a humorous impulse she cannot resist mentioning an anecdote about how names of maids are distorted in Bihar. Cajoling, mocking, reprimanding, Rokeya wants to jolt supine Bengali housewives awake and at the same time deliver a blow to the adamantine community of patriarchal elders.

It seems that Rokeya realised that the most difficult challenge for a colonised nation was to remain cohesive and keep faith against divisiveness injected by the coloniser. 'Sugrihini' ('The Ideal Housewife') was published in 1905, during the tumultuous days of agitation against Lord Curzon's Partition of Bengal. There was a disaffection towards the government and between the communities. The restive atmosphere in the Calcutta and the country occasioned the writer's unexpected and impassioned plea for all Indians to stand united. Here, she exhorts women as wives and mothers to influence their men to not court alienation amongst themselves, showing great confidence in the agency of women. This essay belies its title in directing her readers' attention to concerns far from the sphere of households.

From 'Sugrihini', an excerpt—'Sishu Palon' (Child care)—has been chosen. Rokeya begins this excerpt by commenting: 'This is a very important matter.' She declared that every year 6,26,750 children below the age of twelve died in Bengal. Furthermore, in the dismal atmosphere of dispirited Indians under foreign domination, hopes of reviving a vigorous populace could lie only in a new generation.

Here in the prevailing situation of scarce employment, which had created an atmosphere of distrust between communities and regions, Rokeya finds an avenue for women to intervene. Not included here is the beginning of 'Sugrihini', in which Rokeya beguiles her audience by promising to speak on a topic close to their hearts, teasing them by saying she will not talk about unpopular themes such as equality with men etc. Soon, readers find that it is the spirit of children she wants to nurture, inculcating energy and force, qualities a defeated country needed. The most interesting part is the passionate rhetoric directed at Indians to avoid being isolated in their regional identities, but regard people of all states as their own. 'First, we are Indians—then Muslim, Sikh or anything else. The ideal housewife must inculcate this truth in her family.'

The desperation regarding jobs amongst the ever-increasing numbers of educated men in all communities and regions of India, and the resultant atmosphere of mutual animosity, were matters of deep concern to Rokeya and provoked the outburst above. She often referred to this situation in many different contexts. In *Freedom Fables*, this crisis is addressed in both 'Sugrihini' and 'Chashar Dukkhu' ('The Peasant's Sorrow') from 1921.

In 'Chashar Dukkhu', Rokeya has written a highly polemical article on the eternal poverty of the Indian peasant. She was convinced that the pursuit of employment in service sectors is undesirable because it induces a servile mentality. In 'Niriho Bangali' (Docile Bengalis[16]) of 1903, she encouraged the value of self-reliance whether in farming or in establishing businesses. In this she was in complete accord with the Swadeshi movement then creating great fervour in Bengal. This was the first phase of Swadeshi till it was revived by Gandhi.

In 'Chashar Dukkhu', it is not the urban job-seeker but the Indian peasants who occupy her attention. In solidarity with peasants, Rokeya adopts the rural word 'dukkhu' instead of 'dukkha'. She begins by presenting, in a sentence running ten lines long, all the signs of 'progress' which are glowingly enlisted to sing the praises of British rule in India. To deny such a relentless vision of progress is a traitorous act, declares Rokeya. But hanging above all this, just below the title, are four lines bewailing the naked, scorched hunger of the Indian peasant, mocking those vaunted claims.

The casual inclusion of 'lemonades, gingerades, ice creams, and wallowing "Honourables"', climaxing with scientific food adulterants, reduces these glittering claims to superficiality. This breathless recounting of wonders is internally sabotaged, clashing with the figure of the naked peasant at the head of the article. At present, in 2019, the frequent farmer's rallies point back to the question Rokeya repeatedly hammered in this essay: 'When was the Indian peasant ever happy?'

Many harrowing examples of utter hunger and poverty from Orissa and Rongpur are recounted by the author to prove that the Indian peasant has always been destitute. She refuses to accept the First World War as a reason for their suffering. The self-reliant Indian peasant of the past has been destroyed by the lure of shining 'civilisation'. In this essay, Rokeya points towards a return to indigenous traditions as a solution to rural poverty. Being an activist and no armchair thinker, Rokeya focussed attention on the revival of the Endi silk industry in her native Rongpur, hoping to capitalise on the popularity of 'Assam silk' in Europe. She spent her resources and energy in locating a teacher who could train women and children in this lost skill. Why was this so crucial? It is the old tale of British manufacturing flourishing at the cost of indigenous industry. Specifically, the fame of Assam silk in Europe raised hopes of reviving Endi silk weaving, a rural industry once in the hands of Rongpur women, providing self-sustenance.

An interesting aspect of the Indian Independence movement was how textiles became woven into political discourse and activity. Long before Gandhi made 'khadi' synonymous with nationalism and the Congress, the Swadeshi movement initiated the wearing of rough-spun textiles to counter machine-made foreign cloth. A popular song of the period, then sung in marches by volunteers is:

> Mayer dewa mota kapod mathay tule neyre Bhai
>
> Dindukhini Ma je toder, Tar beshi ar saddho nai.
>
> (Accept with love, my brother, the rough cloth your mother has spun.
>
> Your sad and destitute mother can afford no more than this.)

'Shrishti Totwo' ('The Essence of Creation') from 1920, a humorous caper reminiscent of 'Sultana's Dream', presents the heady enthusiasm aroused by the Satyagraha Movement in the disenchanted voice of Twosti, the Hindu god of creation. Behind the light-hearted raillery of the hostellers, there are glimpses of the tense, repressive atmosphere in a serious phase of the Independence movement, when senior nationalist leaders such as Maulana Azad were interned or imprisoned.

Rokeya's two poems—'The Appeal', 1921 and 'Nirupam Bir', 1922—were written on completely contrasting situations and mood, as well as creatively different standards. 'The Appeal' was written to mock both meek admirers of the imperial power and also the arrogant British-controlled media. The voice of the supplicants is the same voice as Darpanand and his titled cronies from 'Muktiphal'. Rokeya was a mistress of this ironic genre.

'Nirupam Bir' ('Incomparable Warrior') was written on the occasion of the martyrdom of Kanailal Dutta, a young revolutionary sentenced to death for fatally shooting a man who had been providing information to the British on the revolutionaries' identities. This was a poem commissioned by Nazrul Islam, Bengal's revolutionary poet, for his journal *Dhumketu.*

Rokeya shared the admiration of other journalists for the unrepentant spirit of Kanailal, but there is a lack of artistic finesse in this eulogy.

An activist and social reformer with fiercely anti-colonial attitudes, Rokeya could be intensely critical of how the movement for independence was being conducted, but as a writer she had to deploy utmost caution and adroitness in expressing this. In time Rokeya learnt circumspection; the blunt language of her earliest fierce challenge upon orthodoxy was tempered. Exigencies of life were partly responsible for this, as were the compulsions of founding a school for girls of conservative families and its attendant administrative demands.

However, there were times when Rokeya revived her early defiant persona (as in the editorially censured 'Amader Abanati', 1904), choosing to swim against the tide. The Katherine Mayo controversy overwhelmed Indians with anger at the American writer's condemnation of Indian society.[17] In 'Rani Bhikarini' ('The Beggar Queen'), 1927, Rokeya justified Mayo's accusations and used the occasion to turn the guns upon her community, charging them with having reduced the Muslim woman's status to that of a beggar queen.

The-one sided right given to men to divorce a wife by a verbal talaq was another of the injustices which victimised Muslim women and which Rokeya remonstrated against in her writing, as seen in 'Narir Odhikar' ('Rights of Women'). Those were the last words she wrote on behalf of women, on the night she died in 1932. The unfinished article was discovered on her table.

In her fight for women's rights, however, Rokeya did not limit her words for Muslim women, but instead outrightly rejected communalism. A remarkable piece of writing is found in 'Subah Sadek' ('True Dawn'), written in 1931, the year before she died. There is a tone of urgency in this short article. It was a dark time in Bengal. Communal violence and bitter suspicions vitiated the air. Rumours of abduction of Hindu women were floated and 'women protection societies' were organised.

At this moment, Rokeya chose to take a unique stand. She stood for the strength, dignity and individuality of women, refusing to be treated as property which needed protection. She chose to rally the universal community of women against humiliation from men. Rejecting communal identification, she exhorted women to fortify their minds and bodies on their own.

It is this universal community of Indian women that Rokeya draws into her fiction as well, in her construction of 'Mother India'. In 2000 I wrote an essay on the two allegories, titled 'Rokeya Sakhawat Hossain's Gyanphal and Muktiphal: A Critique of the Iconography of the Nation as Mother'.[18] I was struck by the compulsion on Rokeya's part to construct the figure of an ailing, irritable Bharatmata in Kangalini, the deposed queen of Bholapur. In this, she confronts the idol of nationalistic imagination, bejewelled and benign, with its other incarnation: the sometimes idealised, delicate and ascetic Mother India. As an author Rokeya often adopts a contrarian point of view for the sake of truth. The truth she wants to present is that while Indian men invest sentimental worship towards an imagined mother nation, real Indian women lie neglected and suffering.

Rokeya Sakhawat Hossain, who never received any institutionalised education and battled all her life to bring education to women who were confined and deprived, has by a curious irony become part of the syllabi of several universities in India and abroad. Her writings, most often

'Sultana's Dream', are studied from the point of view of gender studies, women's studies, political science, and utopian literature. I expect that *Freedom Fables* will interest scholars in these disciplines to supplement their understanding of that formative text. But above all, these *Fables* and their accompanying essays will be enjoyed by readers who appreciate humour and witty manipulations in fiction and nonfiction, readers who will recognise these gems of allegory and satire from a masterful author.

NOTES

1. Gangopadhay, Arati. *Narimoner Aloy: Dui Shoteker Golpo Sonkolon.* Calcutta: Stri Gobeshona Kendro, 1989, p. vii.

2. Qadir, Abdul. 'Strijatir Abanati' in *Rokeya Rachanabali.* Dhaka: Bangla Academy, 1973, p. 22.

3. Ibid., 'Rasana Puja', p. 229.

4. Ibid., 'Interview with Begum Tarzi', p. 267.

5. Ibid., 'Bongiyo Nari Shiksha Samity', p. 253.

6. Pandita Ramabai (1858–1922) was a reformer and a great Sanskrit scholar in a period when, for the sin of teaching women Sanskrit, her father was driven out of his village. One of her first defiant actions was, being a Brahmin, to marry a man below her caste. She made a living in her youth by giving readings from Sanskrit

texts. She experienced the horror of Indian famines directly, becoming an orphan after losing all the members of her family to it. Unable to reconcile herself to the injustices inherent in Hinduism, she converted to Christianity. She travelled to England and America and was a popular speaker. Returning to India, Ramabai opened a home for widows and orphan girls, where they were educated and trained. She wrote several books in English, including accounts of famines in which she emphasised how women were the worst sufferers.

7.   Brinks, Ellen. 'Feminizing Famine, Imperial Critique: Pandita Ramabai's Famine Essays' *South Asian Review*, Vol. XXV, No. 1, 2004.

8.   In: Qadir, *Introduction*, p. 11.

9.   Lateef, Sayeeda. *Muslim Women in India: Political & Private Realities 1890–1980.* New Delhi: Kali for Women, 1990.

10. Ibid., Lateef, 'Growth of the Indian Women's Movement and the attack on Purdah', p. 74.

11. Jahan, Roushan. *Inside Seclusion: Avarodh Basini of Rokeya Sakhawat Hossain.* Dhaka: Women for Women, 1981.

12. Ghosh, Chitra. *Women Movement Politics in Bengal.* Kolkata: Chatterjee Publishers, 1991.

13. Ray, Bharati. Introduction in *Nari o Poribar: Bamabodhini Potrika.* Kolkata: Ananda Publishers, 2002, p. 7.

14. Amin, Sonia Nishat. *The World of Muslim Women in Colonial Bengal 1876–1939.* Leiden, E.J. Brill, 1976, pp. 219–221.

15. Sathe, Makarand. 'Night Six: Political Plays of the second period: An Introduction to K.P. Khadilkar' in *A*

Socio-Political History of Marathi Theatre: Thirty Nights.
Oxford University Press, 2015, p. 179.

16. In Qadir, *Niriho Bangali*, p. 24.

17. Katherine Mayo: American historian, who was shocked by the inhumane condition of Indian women, particularly Hindus being oppressed by their men. Her book *Mother India* was harsh and unsparing. Indian society was extremely perturbed by her racist ideas and there was a huge outcry against the book. Gandhi in his report called it 'a drain inspector's report.' There has been a reappraisal by Indians recently of Mayo's book. It is now felt that the criticism she levelled at Indian society of that period were for the most part justified.

18. Dutta. Kalyani, 'Rokeya Sakhawat Hossain's Gyanphal and Muktiphal: A Critique of the Iconography of the Nation as Mother', *The Indian Journal of Gender Studies*, December 2000, Vol. 7, No. 2, pp. 203–216.

MUKTIPHAL

The Freedom Tree (1907, 1921)

PART ONE

Kangalini had been ailing for a long time. The lamp of her life was flickering, and those around her thought that she might die soon. She was so poor, she could not afford even a single meal in a day; medicines were out of the question. A tattered quilt was all that covered her body to ward off the bitter chill. Once she had been the Queen of Bholapur. Now she was Kangalini.

As she lay on the green grass under a tree, swarms of mosquitoes and flies harassed her, swarming around her tormented body. Rendered feeble by long illness, she lacked the strength to drive the insects away. Naveen, her young son, sat by her side, playing with the grass. Sometimes, with his small hands, he tried to drive the flies away by waving a palm leaf. Restless and in pain, tears slowly trickled down Kangalini's face.

Naveen wrapped his arms around her neck and said, 'Ma when I grow up, I'll bring a lot of food for you. I'll dress you in Banarasi saris.' Naveen's innocent prattling brought a slight smile to her face and made her forget her suffering.

From the branch of a tree, a bird sang sweetly:

Sons fourteen,
Sorrows umpteen

Kangalini, hearing it, sighed and said, 'That bird is singing a dirge for me. I have a hundred sons, yet I suffer so much. When will the dark night of my sorrows pass?'

Darpananda arrived, his new shoes creaking. Smiling, he declared, 'Ma, your sorrow and poverty will now end. I have ordered a pair of gold ornaments for your feet.'

Kangalini made a great effort to smile and said feebly 'Son, I have to live first. I am dying of hunger.'

Darpananda (annoyed): I don't know how to satisfy your endless hunger. Old people are so troublesome. You refuse to take beef tea and arrowroot biscuits. Then what else will you eat?

Kangalini: I am so poor. A handful of parched rice is all I need.

Darpananda: Oh! This poor barbaric diet! If you refuse to eat cottage cheese, biscuits, marmalade, curdled milk, then go and starve. There is nothing more I can do for you. How is your fever? Here is a dose of quinine.

Kangalini: Quinine won't cure me.

'Die then,' said Darpananda, and left.

Praveen, her other son, came and sat by her side. Lovingly, he patted her hand and said, 'Ma, how thin you have become.'

Out of her deep hurt at Darpananda's behaviour, Kangalini replied, 'No need to worry about that as long as you have plenty of sherry and champagne.'

Praveen: It is your wealthy son Darpananda who drinks sherry and champagne with his friends. Why reproach me? I don't touch spirits. I only eat biscuits. Don't say that we don't care for you. For you, with so many children, it is impossible to die for lack of food and medicines.

The bird called out from the tree:

Sons fourteen,
Sorrows umpteen

Praveen answered the bird, 'No, bird. No more suffering. We will drive away her sorrow.'

Kangalini: Indeed. Death solves all problems. I am ready to die.

Unable to follow the conversation, Naveen stared wide-eyed at his mother's face. He burst into loud wails as soon as he heard his mother speak of death.

Kangalini comforted him. 'Don't cry. I am not going to die. Go play with your brother.'

Naveen: See, I have grown up. Not going to play anymore. Come Dada, let's go and get medicine for Ma.

Praveen: The medicines we get for Ma don't seem to do her any good at all. Ma, are you taking the medicines?

Kangalini: Let it be. Stop worrying about me. It would be better if I die now. May you all have long lives. Let your troubles end with me.

Naveen (tearfully): I am going to be very sad if you die. Dear Ma, I won't let you die.

Kangalini: Wretched child! I can't even die in peace because of you. I wanted to die the day when, once an empress, I became a beggar. With so many helpless children, I couldn't kill myself. It is difficult to die leaving all of you in such a condition. I am not afraid to die. A hundred deaths are preferable to this hateful existence.

Darpananda returned with Ninduk, his brother who liked to find fault with everyone, and said, 'Without medicines or proper diet how can anyone be cured? Ma, you are so simple, you don't understand anything. I want to make your feet shine with golden anklets. But even that doesn't make you happy. I ask you again, please take quinine.'

Kangalini: Look Darpa, don't harass me. I am poor and go around begging for food. Your golden bells will mock me. Medicines will not cure me. To provide what will end this disease is beyond a worthless son like you. Take care of your own comfort and happiness. What more do you need?

Ninduk: Never has Darpananda done anything to make his mother's face shine with pride. Now he wants to make his mother's feet shine with gold chains. Poor fellow. Can't even fulfil that wish! Couldn't even embitter her mouth with quinine!

Kangalini: Ninduk, go. Your words irritate me.

Praveen: Ma, I'll try with all my heart to save you. It's a shame that I cannot cure you of this illness and pain. All my education, my upbringing, is futile.

Ninduk: Bravo! No need to worry. My Praveen is an eloquent speaker. He will succeed with words.

Naveen: I beg you Ma. Tell me, what will cure you?

Kangalini: What use will that be? Will you be able to get the cure?

Praveen: I can get it. I am here for you. Why should you worry?

Kangalini: Then listen. A long time ago, a monk was a guest in my house. He observed that I did not love my sons and my daughters equally. As he was leaving, he said to me, 'You love your sons more and do not care for your daughters. This is wrong. Therefore, you will suffer at the hands of these beloved sons.'

In my heart I had thought, what is the use of lavishing care upon daughters? Will a daughter be able to protect my kingdom of Bholapur? To him I said in agitation 'Master! You have put a curse on me.' He replied, 'How can I curse you? You have to suffer for your karma. Having planted thorns, can one hope to pluck flowers? You have to pay for being the mother of incapable sons and discriminating between your children.'

I fell at his feet and asked again 'When will I be free from the curse?' The sanyasi replied,

'The fruit of freedom grows on a tree on Mount Kailash. The day someone feeds you the fruit of that tree you will be released from the curse.'

Praveen: I'll bring this freedom fruit for you.

Darpa: Kailash is in the kingdom of Mayapur. It is not easy to get this freedom fruit. Ma, you speak of things beyond any man's capacity.

Ninduk: There is nothing a human being can't do.

Praveen: I'll beg for this fruit at the feet of the King of Mayapur. I'll head in the direction of the Emperor's feet immediately.

Kangalini's daughter Shrimati wept, 'Alas! Mother was cursed for neglecting us. Are we not to serve her then? Come Dada, I'll beg at the King's door with you.'

Darpa: Where are you going? Stay where you are. Don't dare to take one step further.

Ninduk (clapping): Shrimati won't hide behind the door anymore. Why should Ma worry? Shrimati will bring the freedom fruit for you.

Shrimati (to herself): Darpa won't let me advance. Ninduk's mockery is intolerable. Only if God is on my side will I be able to help Ma. (Out loud) Ninduk, your sarcasm doesn't matter to me at all. I feel sorry for your twisted ideas.

Ninduk: This is the end! Shrimati feels sorry for me! Oh, how fortunate I am.

Praveen: Shrimati, give me some copies of your songs. I'll need some songs to help me beg.

Shrimati: Let me help you with that. I could sing…

Praveen: No sister, you can't come up to Kailash. Let it suffice that I let you chat with me, read novels, sing prayers. Freedom or equality more than that I cannot allow.

Ninduk: Don't cross your limits, Shrimati. Don't make people laugh at you.

Darpa: Look how good Sumati is. She doesn't step out of the hut.

Shrimati: Sumati is a fool to hide in a corner. Does she have the courage to step out?

Sumati was darning a worn quilt for lack of something to do, and listening. When she heard Shrimati's comments, she thought, A fool or a coward I may be but I'll not venture out in haste without first making myself adequately strong. Has she conquered the world by stepping out? How far has she got? Reading novels and singing with her brother—is that all?

Darpa: We look at Sumati with kindness because she is simple.

Shrimati: Fine. I'll wait to see how long Sumati hides her intelligence. But brother, if you don't let us raise our heads, you are not going to become strong either.

Ninduk: Be quiet Shrimati. No one wants to hear your lecture. Go do your chores. Wash some dishes.

PART TWO

The Pleasure Garden of the King of Mayapur was situated on the top of Mount Kailash. Eighteen thousand demons with open swords in hand patrolled the Garden. Humans, quadrupeds, birds, flies and ants were all barred from entering the Garden.

The old King of Mayapur, having concluded his court work at the end of the day, bade good bye to his officers one by one. Only the Prince, the Prime Minister and a few officials were left. A demon entered and, greeting the king with folded hands, enquired, 'Maharaja, should I speak with caution or with frankness?'

King: Speak without fear.

Demon: On top of Mount Kailash, in the

Pleasure Garden of our Maharaja, the Jewel of the djinn dynasty, there is the tree of Muktiphal.

Prime Minister: Yes. So what?

Demon: On that eternally coveted tree a single fruit is born every hundred years.

Official: Yes, we know. We are aware that a fruit has appeared on the tree again. Say what you have to quickly. No need for a long preamble.

Demon (trembling): There is a rumour that a man-ling has arrived from Bholapur to pluck the Muktiphal.

Crown Prince: Impossible! The report has to be false.

Minister: If the rumour is true, what use are the eighteen thousand demons like you?

Official: If dreaded ones like you keep awake, what have we to fear? Besides, Bholapur is a benighted, insignificant land on earth. Can a human being born there be more powerful than all of you?

Demon: No sir. I only came to inform the Capital. We are all armed and ready. If needed, on the earth of Kailash will flow fountains of human blood.

Minister: Spoken like a hero. You may leave now.

Prince (rising from his seat): I have something to say.

All: Please speak.

Prince: I don't have the audacity to speak about administrative affairs. But I have to remonstrate against the comments of the Prime Minister. He showed lack of wisdom in encouraging the demons to create rivers of human blood. There is nothing heroic on the part of a mighty, powerful nation like ours in destroying Bholapur's emasculated race. On the other hand, the King of Mayapur is celebrated all over the world of the djinns as compassionate and just. What will the rulers of our neighbouring djinn kingdoms say if human blood is spilt inside the Kingdom of Mayapur? Won't all Paristhan call us cowards instead of heroes?

Minister: The Prince's comments are entirely rational. Human blood will disgrace our reputation. All Paristhan will be defiled too. But the defiance on the part of Man is intolerable. They have come to take away Muktiphal. How do we stop them?

Official: I am sure the Prince has thought of some way.

King: That was a substantial argument, son. You have demonstrated the imminent disgrace to

Mayapur, the crown of Paristhan. Now, do what is necessary to accomplish the task at hand. If you succeed, I'll give up the kingdom in your hands and retire to meditate.

All: 'Kill the snake but don't let the stick break'—that is the kind of solution we need.

Prince: It is said that the human race is extremely ignorant while the djinns and the demons are skilled in the science of illusion. It should be easy to charm the ignorant, insensitive human beings by magic. If Muralidhar, the erudite magician, were to play some melancholy, sympathetic music on his enticing flute, the men will dance in step to his tune. Then the other djinn musicians will tempt them by offering to take them to Muralidhar. When the men accept, the djinns and demons will easily mislead them.

The assembly welcomed the Prince's proposal with applause.

Thereafter the Prince, in several secret meetings with all chief demons, guards and the scholar magician Muralidhar, made his plans.

In the end, it was decided that the demons would not harm the humans in any way. They would keep an eye on human activities and inform Mayapur.

Many years ago, the slopes of Mount Kailash had been planted with thorns. The djinns, paris and demons moved to and fro in magic vehicles.

PART THREE

Laek was exhausted after having nursed his mother day and night. He had taken no care of his own need for food and sleep; consequently, his health had suffered. He sat silently near his mother and softly caressed her feet. Recognising her son's touch, Kangalini opened her eyes and said, 'Laek! Here you are. Of course. Is there anyone else who would care for the pain of his unfortunate mother? Well son, all your care is not going to save me. I am not going to be cured of this disease unless I have the Muktiphal.'

Shrimati approached with some food on a small plate and pleaded, 'Ma, you've become so weak. Eat a little bit, so that you can get some strength.'

Kangalini: Won't be able to swallow anything before I taste Muktiphal.

Laek: Who knows when Praveen will return with the Muktiphal. Here you have almost shrunk into the earth. No strength left even to drive away flies and mosquitoes.

Shrimati: Ma might die before Dada arrives with the fruit. Alas! What is the use of the cure arriving after the patient has died?

Kangalini: Don't worry about me, dear. I won't die. If I die, who will be left in the world to suffer? Fasting, ailing, tolerating unending taunts and humiliations, I still have to live on. You see this worn piece of cloth? One end of it is in the hands of the djinns of Mayapur and the other end I have wrapped round my waist to protect my modesty like the miserable, half-disrobed Draupadi. But in the midst of all the humiliations, I have to live on. Allah! Have mercy on me.

At this moment Laek collapsed, overcome by pain. Startled, Shrimati ran up to him. Unaware that her sibling was about to die, Shrimati looked helplessly at her mother, 'Look Ma! What's happened to Dada?'

Somehow Kangalini struggled and managed to sit up, lifting her dying son onto her lap as she began to weep. She wailed loudly 'Laek! Laek! Son! You are leaving me. Alas! You were my comfort in these hard days. You took my death onto yourself.'

With eyes almost closed, Laek said 'Ma, don't be so sad. I thank God that I am dying in the service of my mother. Can there be a greater glory than this? He who dies for his own sake dies painfully; but one who lays down his life for the sake of his mother…' He died, leaving his words unfinished.

Kangalini: This is why I told Laek not to be a nurse to me. He caught my incurable, infectious disease and died. Alas! It is beyond anyone to release me from this curse. I loved my sons more than my daughters. Spoilt by such love, one became Darpananda the boastful; one became an ingrate; one became Ninduk the censurer; another one a mother-hater. Laek, the golden one, the only one fit to be called a human being, was seized by death. I have no more hope, no faith left now.

Shrimati: Ma, don't let despair madden you. You still have my brothers, Dhiman, Praveen, Naveen, and I am there too, your humble attendant. You can't give up hope. There has to be an end to your suffering. That is what I think.

Kangalini: I find it unbearable that in spite of Darpananda's immense wealth, I am destitute.

Naveen stood next to where Laek lay and kept calling his name. When Laek didn't answer, he rushed to Shrimati and asked 'Didi, why is Laek Dada sleeping?'

Shrimati: Our Laek Dada isn't sleeping. He has become immortal.

Naveen: I want to be immortal too Didi.

Kangalini: Fine. Don't chatter now. Go and play.

Naveen: It's no fun playing alone. When will Praveen Dada return?

Kangalini: Praveen will bring back the Muktiphal.

Naveen: Dada won't be able to get the Muktiphal. Let me go get it.

Shrimati: You have grown up now. Good, go then and get it. We will wait for you.

PART FOUR

Every day, Praveen sat at the base of Mount Kailash and wrote drafts of an appeal addressed to the King of Mayapur. A neat seven maunds of ink had been spent in writing this appeal. Reeds having been used as pens, all the reed beds of the kingdom had been exhausted. Paper had run short, so now the appeal was written on the leaves of the Arum lily. The boars, fearing a famine of Arum lilies, had sent a petition to God, the provider of food.

Praveen sent his appeals to the King by the hands of a different demon every day, but had received no reply so far. The magical singers told him, 'Please remain assured, the King will pluck the fruit with his own hands to give to you.'

Praveen (to Mayavi): I am not worried. But when I return home, Darpananda will taunt Mother, 'Where is the fruit brought by your gifted son?' And now that Naveen has grown up, I can't stand his goading. He just doesn't give me any peace. Keeps bothering me with questions all the time.

Mayavi: Can't you somehow trick Naveen?

Praveen: Well, if I had twenty-five to thirty demon guards with me, it would not be difficult to teach Naveen a lesson.

Mayavi: That is if we can catch Naveen. He is very arrogant. Never comes to the demons to beg for the fruit. Doesn't come anywhere near us. Keeps his distance. As for Darpananda's taunts, he is under our control. He wants to turn into a monkey. Needs a tail for that. To acquire that tail he is paying court to a djinn. Once we tie him up with that tail, he will not be able to move. Or speak a word. This year when the Prince is crowned, Darpananda will be bound by his tail.

Praveen (aside): I could have acquired a tail as well. But now Naveen will laugh at me, so I have to hide my desire for a tail. Darpananda suffers from no shyness and so doesn't mind the tail. (Loudly) Look, here comes Darpananda with his friends.

Mayavi: Let him come. We have no objections. He is our friend too.

Darpananda (prostrating himself before Mayavi): I trust you are well.

Mayavi: Come and take a seat. What news do you bring?

Darpananda: All is well with us. I hope the Maharaja, the Jewel of the djinn race, remembers the matter of a tail for me?

Mayavi: Oh, he has definitely kept it in mind. But there is one thing. Are you too a claimant for the Muktiphal?

Darpananda: No! No, sir! Am I mad? Any work that displeases our worshipful King of Mayapur is beyond me. About that matter you must ask my twin Praveen.

Praveen (nervously): What have I done? Am I trying to seize the Muktiphal by force? I have only begged humbly, with folded hands, at the King's lotus-like feet. The munificent one will grant it to me if he wishes.

Mayavi: That is right. Be assured of the King's generosity. The King will certainly fulfil your wishes. It will take a few years yet for the Muktiphal to ripen. As soon as it is ripe, we will ourselves bring it over to you.

Darpananda: We have no need for that fruit. Let my old mother die. My hundred and six friends and I are devoted to the King of the djinns. So, we don't want the Muktiphal. (Addressing his friends) Sing that song of praise you have composed.

A hundred and seven people led by Darpananda sang out to the accompaniment of a sitar:

Together hundred and seven are we.
All true and deep djinn devotees.
Deep in the heart
Flows ever so fast,
Shaking the horizon with its roar,
A waterfall of djinn love, cool and clear.
We have no care
For siblings or mother.
If mother's starving to death, I can't wait.
Hundred and seven, steadfast in King djinn faith

Pleased by the song, Mayavi applauded, 'Bravo Darpananda! Bravo! You are all very intelligent. You understand clearly where your wellbeing lies. Why worry about the old lady?'

Darpananda: No. I am not concerned at all about my old mother, as long as I am contented.

Praveen (aside): That wretched Naveen won't let me live in peace. Dhiman is harassing me too. He says we can't rest easy till we acquire the Muktiphal. I only meant to comfort Mother when I said I will bring the fruit. But this Naveen has taken it seriously and thrown himself at it. (To all) You are right, brother. Self-preservation is the law of nature.

Mayavi: Look, don't worry about the fruit. We are preserving the fruit for ailing Kangalini. We have no interest in it.

Darpananda and Praveen: Oh! Is that so? You are all so compassionate.

Mayavi: Praveen! We are all very fond of you. You must stay close to us at all times.

Praveen (softly): Certainly. You can keep an eye on me.

And so Mayavi left. Ninduk, hiding behind a tree, had overheard the conversation. Now he came forward and addressed Praveen laughingly, saying 'So Praveen, you got the Muktiphal?'

Praveen, embarrassed, answered, 'Haven't got it yet. Hope to get it soon. Don't be impatient. I'll certainly bring the Muktiphal for Mother. Naveen has cleared out some of the forest near the Mountain. Let me proceed along that path and find out how much further Mount Kailash is.'

Darpananda: Beware! It's not safe to step on that road. If the demons find out there will be trouble.

Praveen: But Naveen wants me to build stairs in that direction. He is hard at work uprooting the thorns. Shouldn't I even go and have a look?

Darpananda: Go and look. But Naveen is so terribly heedless; he is going to get into trouble.

Smirking, Ninduk said, 'Praveen and Naveen's ascent of Kailash and plucking the Muktiphal, all this will be accomplished without a hitch. The demons are sound asleep and snoring.'

Praveen: I am not careless like Naveen. I know how to hide. I keep both sides happy. To Naveen I promise, yes, I will build a staircase. To the demons I say, let me advance a little bit further. As soon as you throw down the Muktiphal I'll catch it.

Ninduk and Darpananda burst into laughter. Praveen felt slightly abashed.

PART FIVE

All the courtiers were present in the court of Mayapur. Being unwell, the King was unable to attend court and was resting in the inner quarters of Pari-mahal. The Prince was conducting the affairs of the kingdom.

An official commented to Muralidhar, 'Mankind doesn't seem to have been charmed by your flute.'

Muralidhar: My honourable friend seems to be unaware of the news from the earth. Mankind has certainly been charmed.

Official: Praveen's words and work differ. While he says to us that he will only beg at the King's feet, in reality he is building stairs along with Naveen to climb up to Mount Kailash. Is Muralidhar seized of this matter?

Second official: That is a matter of concern.

Muralidhar: You are all so ignorant. Praveen's stair-building is only a game. The staircase is being made with stone and that too not more than one step in a year.

Prince: No need for this argument. Call the lead singer and ask.

In a moment the lead singer arrived by magic chariot.

Muralidhar: Tell us poet, what news do you bring of the earth? Has Praveen left with the Muktiphal?

Singer: If Praveen had left with the Muktiphal, then why would so many demons be present at Mount Kailash as guards? But it's true, mankind might succeed in climbing up to Mount Kailash in the future.

Minister: Impossible. Completely impossible.

Prince: How did the singer come to know that Praveen will succeed in climbing Mount Kailash?

Singer: Praveen won't be able to ascend Mount Kailash. The poor man was so far contented with writing his appeals and making speeches. But now, egged on by Naveen, he wants to build stairs. Naveen doesn't let him sit idle. This Naveen is the cause of all the trouble.

Minister: Even so, there is no cause for apprehension. Unless Naveen, Praveen, Dhiman, Ninduk, Darpananda all try together, they are not going to succeed in climbing Mount Kailash. But they are never going to be united with each other.

Therefore, we have no need to worry. Besides, Kangalini is not going to get the Muktiphal unless she sacrifices her sons. But she loves her sons and won't be able to sacrifice them.

Singer: True. But Laek has willingly laid down his life.

All (shocked): Really? Has that weak, timid son of Kangalini finally given up his hold on life?

Singer: Yes. Laek's sacrifice is real. We witnessed it ourselves.

A courtier: Then it is wrong to deprive Kangalini of her Muktiphal.

Minister (sarcastically): Really? Then let us remove the eighteen thousand demon sentries from Mount Kailash. Let Man effortlessly, without any hindrance, eat the unripe Muktiphal and find out how it tastes.

Many voices (together): No! No! You mustn't do that! The simple heart of Man doesn't understand what is good for him and what is not. They are incapable of saving themselves. Our kind and soft hearts cannot stand aside and watch them harming themselves by eating the raw Muktiphal.

Contemplating the imminent sufferings of the human race, all present in the court shed tears to flood many pitchers.

Prince (controlling his tears by a valiant effort): Does the singer believe that imprudent Naveen will succeed in ascending the mountain and pluck the Muktiphal?

Singer: No, I don't believe that. Only, when I see Naveen bragging and jumping around, I can't stop laughing.

Minister: According to astrology, till such time as Kangalini's daughters assist their brothers, no one will be able to take away the Muktiphal. And you are all aware how insignificant and useless Kangalini's daughters are.

All: Then we can rest easy for many years.

Minister: Absolutely! Take the matter of Naveen and Praveen building stairs. Naveen says 'Let's build a step higher.' Praveen says 'No. Let's go down and build one a little lower.' Naveen says 'Let's climb up.' Praveen says 'Let's climb down.' The brothers keep bickering like this.

A courtier (laughing): Hearing the vaunts of Kangalini's useless sons, a friend of mine asked us to be wary. If someone becomes so nervous on hearing empty speeches, then he will simply faint on hearing the warbling of a koel.

The courtiers laughed uproariously.

Minister: Truly, there is no need for anxiety. A few mischievous demons are trying to annoy us by spreading rumours.[1]

Prince: Now we are reassured. But it would not do to be too relaxed. Let Muralidhar keep playing his flute as before.

Thereafter Muralidhar began playing his flute with doubled, even tripled enthusiasm. The dulcet tones of his magic flute lulled the seven seas into forgetting the roar of the waves; the constant wind became stilled; trees, things animate and inanimate—all pricked up their ears. The birds in the sky forgot to sing sweetly. How then could Praveen withstand the music of the flute? He was after all only a human being.

PART SIX

In the valley of Kailash, Naveen, Praveen, Dhiman and Ninduk were all present. Dhiman was urging the construction of a staircase while Naveen, ignoring his instructions, was hurriedly assembling a ladder of new bamboo poles. Very slowly, Praveen was collecting the materials needed to build a stone staircase. Ninduk had no intention of working himself; he was there only to find fault with all his eager, labouring brothers. Whenever he found a chance, he shot taunts at Naveen, or thoroughly confused Praveen by raining down sarcastic comments on him. Thus were the four brothers engaged in the work of serving their mother.

Naveen (addressing Praveen): Dada, your procrastination is so annoying. Even today you have not finished collecting your material. When will the staircase be completed so that you can climb up? You are not fit to fetch the Muktiphal.

Praveen: What! I have been looking after Mother for the last twenty-two to twenty-three years, and am trying to climb to the top of Mount Kailash. And you, a stripling, hardly two to three years old in this work, dare say, 'It is not up to you to fetch the Muktiphal'! Do you think you are going to be able to climb up by that feeble bamboo ladder? First, the ladder is going to crumble as soon as you to step on it; second, how are you going to protect yourself from wind, rain and hail?

Naveen: Won't you get wet climbing up the stone staircase?

Praveen: Am I foolish like you that I would move without considering every step of the way?

Under every step I am going to build a little room. When needed and if there is lightning, I'll hide inside it.

Dhiman: A lifetime will be wasted in such considerations of your own comfort and safety without anything being achieved.

Praveen: Do you have any idea how many thorns there are on this route?

Dhiman: You can't retreat for fear of thorns. Not thorns alone; on these hilly, forested tracks there are snakes, scorpions. On further heights there will be hailstorms and thunder. You have to proceed without thinking about them.

Naveen: No. I won't care for them. With a weapon to beat the wind in my hand what is there to fear? (Grabbing Praveen's hand) Come, Dada, let's go.

Praveen (aside): I can't do it. (Loudly) My leg shakes, your ladder is so weak.

Naveen: Use the Bykata weapon as a lever and leap up.

Praveen: Got to hide that Bykata. The demon guards will go mad if they see it. And certainly, my appeals have to go with me.

Naveen: The Arum lily leaves your appeals are written on are together equal in weight to the volume of seven carts. Impossible to carry all that up. No brother, no need for appeals or pleas—

Praveen: No! Naveen, listen to the thunder. We will get drenched halfway up.

Naveen: What's the harm in getting wet?

At this moment, the three magical singers arrived.

First singer: Where are you going?

Praveen: Naveen wants to climb up to the top of Mount Kailash.

Ninduk (to himself): Praveen is so cunning. So quick to report Naveen's travel plans, keeping it secret that he too is bound that way.

Second singer: Going to use that ladder to climb up? Are you mad? What use is that Bykata weapon? You have to leave that behind.

Third singer: Come, we'll show you the way. There is a very nice hard road.

Praveen: Come along, Naveen. They'll show us the way.

Naveen: No. We won't take help from others.

Praveen: I have heard that Muralidhar lives in the kingdom of Mayapur. And that like the Wishing Tree, he fulfils the prayers of all.

First singer: Yes. If you want we could take you to him. He will give you the Muktiphal with his own hands.

Praveen: Well Naveen, won't you come?

Naveen: I have heard of the generosity of many such Wishing Tree people. But we cannot depend any longer on alms.

Praveen: Make no mistake, there is no more generous person than Muralidhar.

Naveen: I don't believe it.

From a distance, the strains of a flute were heard.

Whatever is your heart's wish
will be granted by the flautist.
So come, O Praveen.
Go away, Naveen,
Your face I abhor.
Praveen, come closer.
Muktiphal why do you desire,
who have heaps of fruits and flowers?
The sun do you crave?
That too will you get,
And a necklace of stars.
Ask not for moonlight.

The moon itself will I bring.
Come quickly Praveen.

Praveen: What more do you want, Naveen? Let's go with them.

Naveen: I won't go. Muralidhar hasn't asked for me. Wouldn't have gone even if he had.

'Stay then. I'm off.' Saying this, Praveen left, abandoning Naveen. The djinns took him away by twisting paths, deep into the forest.[2] They impressed upon Praveen that if he followed their example, he would acquire mukti and moksha— he would have it all. The djinns might even grant him power over all Earth.

Praveen (overcome by emotion): You'll make me the King of the world and all its seas! Oh, I hardly deserve all your kindness.

Mayavi: Not only the Earth and its seas; one by one we will give you all the kingdoms of the solar system. The world of Saturn is somewhat huge. We will have to make great efforts to conquer it.

Praveen: Oh. Your utter kindness kills me. I will be gratified if you make me a minister now, if not a king yet.

At this point, a voice rang out. 'Dada! Dada!

Where are you? How far do I have to go to find my brother?'

Praveen: Oh, what a nuisance! Naveen has come here as well. I am not going to answer.

Swiftly looking around him, Praveen hid himself inside a cave. Naveen entered the tunnel and saw Praveen.

Naveen: Dada? What are you doing in this tunnel? I am exhausted, having searched for you everywhere. For three days I have been walking all day and night till now, when I found you.

Praveen: You want to climb up to Kailash on that ladder. I can't do it.

Naveen: All right Dada. I'll do whatever you say. Come, we will follow your way. I'll only take my native Bykata.

Praveen (aside): You can say what you like but I am not letting you attach yourself to me again. (out loud) It's because of you that my staircase couldn't be finished. By now I would have been halfway up.

Naveen: Nothing is lost. Build your stairs. Let's take along all bricks and stones.

¤

Very reluctantly Praveen, with Naveen in tow, advanced a little up the mountain and began building a few steps of the stairs. At the same time a chorus of the invisible magical singers sang sweetly:

Hear, O hear, the music of the flute.
Waste not your time in useless pursuit.
Bring all your petitions,
Walk with us in unison.
We will take you to Bansidhar.
The music of the flute, oh hear.

Praveen lost himself in the music. He thought: With Naveen with me, I can't retreat; I can't approach Muralidhar in Kadamtola. Naveen shows no signs of leaving me alone. What shall I do? Let me give Naveen a push and throw him down.

Giving up on building the staircase, Praveen gave Naveen a hard push. Unable to judge the strength of the push, he lost his own footing and fell down too. Both men rolled down to the valley below. They regained their footing without delay and dusted themselves off.

Ninduk burst into laughter and clapped. Dhiman didn't laugh; he was very upset.

Praveen remonstrated and told Naveen, 'It was your fault we fell.'

Naveen: What! Dada, you pushed me.

Praveen: I don't know about that. You made me fall.

Naveen: This is like a thief accusing the judge! If you hadn't pushed me how could we fall?

Praveen: If what you say is true, then how could I fall since I pushed?

Naveen: Because you couldn't control the force of the push.

Praveen: The world will testify that the one who pushes can't fall.

Naveen: Everyone has understood your trick. It is you who pushed and made us fall.

Praveen: Quiet! You liar! I have been building the stairs for these twenty-two to twenty-three years and now you say I am responsible for our fall.

Naveen: You are not going to get power just by abusing me in this crude manner. Everyone knows who is lying.

Praveen: You have destroyed the labour of twenty-three years. Alas! I have been looking after Ma for these last twenty-three years. The result of all my care, hard work destroyed in a second. Come, let us go to Ma.

Naveen: Yes, let's go. Ma knows what each of her sons is like.

PART SEVEN

Kangalini was very seriously ill. There was hardly any hope for her to survive. Shrimati and Sumati were engaged in nursing their mother. The skeletal form and pale face of her mother made Shrimati weep. Sometimes, she imagined that her brother would arrive with the Muktiphal at any moment. The fall of a leaf or any small noise would fill Shrimati's heart with hope: 'There! My brother is here.'

Hoping against hope, Sumati kept awake throughout the long night of the month of Paush. Then it was morning. That day Naveen, Praveen and others were scheduled to return with the Muktiphal. It was a day of joy. Wiping her mother's face and hands, Sumati changed her tattered clothes and sat down at the door of their worn-down hut, staring unblinkingly at the road and waiting.

Before his brothers could make their appearance, Ninduk ran up and informed his sisters that Praveen was returning with the Muktiphal.

Sumati (excited): Oh, I can't believe it. Swear that it is true, brother.

Ninduk: I swear by your hair it is true. Dhiman is bringing with him a gold plate full of food and Naveen's bringing a sari from Varanasi for Ma.

Shrimati: Oh, let them come soon. Ma is half dead with sickness and sorrow. Oh, when will my brothers come?

Ninduk: Don't be impatient Shrimati. There, see, Praveen is approaching.

Spotting Praveen from a distance, Sumati came running. 'Why Dada, where is the fruit?'

Praveen: Ask your favourite brother Naveen. I could have got it if Naveen hadn't arrived.

Naveen: Then why didn't you get it all these years?

Sumati: What did you achieve in the end? Ma is about to breathe her last. How could you have so little shame as to return empty-handed?

Praveen: It's no use blaming me. It is all Naveen's fault.

Naveen: God knows, it is entirely my brother's fault. He threw me down the ladder.

Praveen: Naveen was ready for a fall from the beginning.

Naveen: Dada had fixed it beforehand to knock me down.

Praveen: Don't lie and make your load of sins heavy.

Naveen: To tell lies at your age...

Dhiman: Ma is at death's door. Is this a proper time for your quarrel? Isn't it shameful enough that you returned unsuccessful?

Kangalini (to herself): O Earth, split in two. Let me hide myself in you. Shrimati dear, your brothers are tired. Tell them to rest.

Sumati: Ninduk Dada, tell me truly. Who knocked down whom?

Ninduk: What can I say, sister? The one who becomes restless at the sound of the flute, who is invited by Muralidhar, the erudite magician, to sit next to him under the shade of the Kadamba— it was him, absentmindedly he pushed and both fell down.

Naveen: Now Ninduk Dada has spoken the truth.

Praveen: Were all my years of labour a futile waste?

Shrimati: We don't know what you did in those twenty-three years. All we want to see is the result of your work. Who cleared out the deep forest which stretched from the door of Ma's hut to the foot of Mount Kailash?

Dhiman: It has taken Naveen twenty-three years to clear out that dense forest.

Ninduk: All Praveen did was sit in that secluded forest and write petitions.

Sumati: Let it be. Watch out! Ma's hut has caught fire. Come on, let's put it out.

Kangalini lay on the floor, the earth soaked with her tears. Her heart was shattered in shame, hurt and disappointment. As Sumati tried to pull her out of the burning hut, she protested, 'Sumati, don't drag me around anymore. Let me burn to death.'

Shrimati: No, Ma! How can you die while we are still around?

Kangalini: Wretched girl! Don't you know that I won't be freed of the curse till I eat the Muktiphal? Why torture me just to keep me alive in body?

Naveen: Ma, dear Ma! Don't be angry. I will

try again to get the Muktiphal. I couldn't climb Mount Kailash this time. I'll try again.

Shrimati and Sumati: We'll come along this time. Is the road inaccessible?

Naveen: Not inaccessible throughout. We can climb up part of the way by a ladder.

Shrimati: I understand. No need for the ladder. Let's go, Naveen. We shouldn't delay any longer.

Ninduk: Strange, Shrimati! Naveen has at least got hold of a ladder. You don't want to take any kind of support.

Shrimati: Why Dada? I depend on my own two feet. I am going to pull myself up by the hilly creepers and plants. When that won't do, then I'll crawl. In whatever way I can, I'll climb.

Praveen: Where it is too steep, how will you climb?

Ninduk: Then both sisters will try to climb together.

Sumati: Why are you so full of taunts, Dada? There has to be a way. Nothing lasts forever. Either you are cured or you die. An illness does not last forever.

Dhiman: Let's not waste time in words. We will all start on the journey again.

Praveen: Yes, let's go. I'll collect a few petitions and follow.

Shrimati: I am going to let down my hair. Till we all fetch the Muktiphal for mother I am not going to tie my hair. O almighty God, help us.

Kangalini: What is this I see! My tender-bodied, butter-soft daughters have sacrificed their well-being, all worldly pleasures, to dedicate themselves to my service! Since Shrimati and Sumati have now determined to join their brothers, I have confidence that perhaps my long night of despair may end. Perhaps at long last my children will bring Muktiphal for me. Hope tantalises.

NOTES

1. Rokeya's note: Usually, Mussalmans do not believe in ghosts, but believe in the existence of djinns, paris (fairies) and demons. It is said that the djinns envy Man but in some places the djinns and paris marry humans. The demons too are hostile to the djinns. According to the writer, the demons, though huge and very powerful, are under the control of the djinns. It is common to say 'King djinn and worker demon'; or 'the private quarter of such and such pari has a demon guard and protector'. Whatever it might be, the demons are successful in satisfying their enmity by harassing the djinns any chance they get.

2. Rokeya's note: It is said djinns are unwilling to be subdued by humans; So, they try to impede people who are on a quest. Sometimes they try to frighten a devotee by assuming terrifying shapes. At other times they skilfully beguile them into a forest to destroy their mission. Even Vyasdev, when misled in his meditation, regretted to his Goddess,

> I wasted away in your contemplation.
>
> What did you gain by deceiving Vyas?
>
> What a clever trick Devi Durga played in granting Vyas the donkeys Varanasi!

GYANPHAL

The Tree of Knowledge (1907, 1921)

In the beginning, Adam and Hava lived in the Garden of Eden. In heaven they lived in complete bliss as guests of God Almighty. They wanted for nothing. All that the Almighty had asked of them was to not eat the fruit of one particular tree.

One day, as she wandered down the saffron-scented paths of the heavenly Garden, Hava came to rest under the shade of the forbidden tree. With enraptured eyes she observed the beauty of the Garden. Listening to the sweet chirping of the birds in the trees, she absentmindedly plucked some fruits from the tree and ate them.

As soon as she ate the fruit, knowledge filled her mind. She realised that though they lived in royal splendour as state guests, she did not have even a rag to cover her beautiful body. Instantly she covered herself in her long, knee-length tresses. Her heart felt heavy with a strange, new kind of pain.

At that moment Adam arrived. Hava asked him to eat the fruit in her hand. Knowledge came to Adam the moment he ate the fruit. In every layer of his heart he realised his miserable condition. Could this be heaven? This loveless, idle existence—was this heavenly bliss? He realised that he was a prisoner of the state. He had no power to step beyond the limits of the Garden of Eden.[1] He lived in a magnificent palace built of bricks of gold and silver, and paths laid with powdered coral and pearls. Yet he possessed not a single thing he could call his own—not even a piece of cloth. What kind of luxury was this?

Ignorance, which had made everything seem a dream of heavenly bliss, was now shattered. Sharp and keen was the awakening of knowledge. In place of enchantment and contentment, there was a feeling of consciousness and disquiet. He said to Hava, 'What illusion kept us oblivious for so long? How could we have been so happy in this state?'

Hava replied, 'Indeed. This place is a diadem of beauty. Fragrant saffron carpeting the flower beds like grass; graceful creepers adorned with diamond buds; emerald shoots on trees tipped with flowers of ruby—delightful to one's eyes but unfulfilling of the yearnings of the heart. Water like nectar of flowers from the Kausar Lake satisfies one's thirst but does it meet the aspiration of one's heart? What need have we for all this heavenly wealth?'

Desire for some unimagined transformation made them restless. On a visit to the Garden, the Almighty found the couple hiding from him behind some trees. The Lord called out to them but they, out of grief, hurt and shame, could not confront their master. Being omniscient, the Almighty was aware of everything. He became angry and said, 'You want freedom? Go then. Scram! Go down to earth and discover the pleasures of freedom.'

The duo fell that day, and arrived on earth. Here they went through various shades of experience, successfully undergoing tests of poverty and sufficiency, ailments, happiness and sorrow, eventually achieving a proper conjugal existence. Hava loved her daughters, so she blessed them with long life, contented homes, and endless store of love in their hearts. Adam's favourites were his sons but his will was not very strong so he did not grant any special boons to his sons.

Due to Hava's blessing, all her daughters, from birth, doubled their strength and lived four times longer than usual. Adam's dear scions, once born, were spoiled so much that they suffered two times more illnesses and died in numbers four times more than the norm! If natural causes did not kill them, they killed each other in wars. Some rotted in prisons; others suffered various other kinds of troubles.

When being expelled from Heaven, Hava had thrown her half-eaten fruit down to earth as well. A huge tree grew from its seed in the eastern part of the world. In time, the sapling became loaded with fruits and flowers, but at that time the people of that country did not know how to take care of the tree. Piles of ripe fruit lay under the tree, and jackals and crows filled their bellies with them. The remaining fruit piled high near the banks of the nearby Shanta River, and some rolled down into the river. The water of the river, flavoured with the juice of the knowledge fruit, fell into a great sea—and on the other side of this sea lay Paristhan.

The djinn people of Paristhan were very good-looking but, with the exception of physical beauty, theirs was a land where little else was found in plenty. Forests of makal[2] covered their country. There was an acute shortage of adequate foodstuff. Innovative techniques, great care, hard work: nothing the djinns did was able to secure satisfactory results from their harsh, infertile land. The djinns and Paris[3] lived in pleasure palaces as splendid as celestial Amaravati; they were surrounded by innumerable objects of luxury; and great was their wealth. Yet, they suffered from fiery hunger in their bellies. Such are the curious games destiny plays upon us.

Once, a few djinns were bathing in the ocean. Overcome by hunger, they swallowed some saline ocean water. The moment the water was swallowed, the curtain of ignorance fell away from their minds. The complex problem of food, which had hitherto kept them preoccupied, was instantly resolved. Knowledge brought them the power of perception and they could see a way out.

That day, the djinns determined that they would travel to many lands for trade. Accordingly, they loaded their ships with makal fruit and sailed. The ships of the djinns, after wandering past many lands, finally arrived at a port on the shores of a huge ocean.

The sight of the prosperous cities of

Kanakadwipa transfixed the eyes of the djinn traders. They had a firm conviction that there was no country as wealthy as their country and that in their hands a fistful of dust would turn into gold. But the earth of Kanakadwipa yielded treasure. Here there were many trees bearing delicious fruits, the mango foremost among them. The civilised and saintly inhabitants of the land, a race of golden-bodied people, lived mainly on fruits.

The djinn traders thought: Let's begin by misleading them. Thereafter, they exchanged makal fruits with some mangoes of the Sonamukhi and Andharmanik varieties from the Kanakadwipa people. In this way, every year they brought ships loaded with makal and returned with ships full of mangoes. In time this trade flourished. But as their trade prospered, in Kanakadwipa there occurred a shortage of mangoes.

The djinns spread from the cities to the villages in search of mangoes. They saw the autumn fields in the villages bursting with golden paddy. The sight made them sigh. 'These people do not know what it is to be hungry.'

After a little hesitation, the traders asked a peasant to exchange rice for makal. The peasant failed to understand the djinns' language.

Moreover, a group of small plump children gazed in wonder at the handsome faces of the traders. The traders thought to themselves, 'What a farce! We seem to have become a source of entertainment to these peasant children.'

In time, the traders were able to convey their wishes to the peasant. The peasant refused to trade rice in exchange for makal, but his son spoke up, 'Oh, give it to them. They are starving. We have plenty of rice.'[4]

In Paristhan, a land advanced in scientific knowledge, the number of merchant ships kept increasing every year. Now that there was no longer a lack of food, nothing troubled the paris. Whenever they pleased, they came to visit Kanakadwipa on their magic chariots. They became very friendly with the women of Kanakadwipa. The Kanaka women began trying to ape the dress of the paris. All that remained was for them, too, to sprout two wings like the paris.

In the beginning, makal used to be imported in one or two ships. Later countless ships loaded with makal arrived three or four times a year to Kanakadwipa. Loads and loads of rice began to be exported to Paristhan while in Kanakadwipa, the fascination for makal grew so strong that peasants were unable to control themselves. No longer did the peasant store rice for the whole year. It came to pass that rice harvested today could, and would, be exchanged for makal the next day. And soon, the demon named Famine came and settled down in Kanakadwipa to stay.

A remarkable incident occurred during this trade of makal. A wonderful guava tree had grown near the coast of a huge sea in Paristhan. The guavas shared some characteristics of the knowledge fruit, having been nourished by sea water steeped in the juice of that fruit. The djinns and the paris used to collect the guavas with great care and keep them for their own use. However, once, while the traders were busy loading makal in the ships, some guavas happened to fall off the tree into the ships. The guavas were thus imported to Kanakadwipa along with the makal and were sold.

A few fortunate inhabitants of Kanakadwipa ate the guavas of Paristhan and threw away the seeds. From those seeds, guava trees grew in Kanakadwipa.

¤

A hundred years passed.

With the help of the guavas, a few gentlemen of Kanakadwipa now woke from their dreams. And what a bitter awakening it was, after such a long interval of charmed sleep, lasting several hundred years! It was as if sight had been restored, ending blindness, only for them to plunge once more into utter darkness when they saw what was around them. With astonishment, these people of Kanakadwipa looked around and found that, in exchange for makal, the djinns had taken away all that the country possessed. Now, like leeches, the djinns were engaged in sucking out the last few remaining drops of blood. Observing the misery of the people, their hearts were wrenched.

Now no mango orchards existed; no delicious fruits grew on trees, and fields were bereft of golden harvest; the fertile earth had turned to dust. Every home resounded with cries for food. The peasants were no longer full of the glow of health; their bodies were now skeletal, clad in torn rags. The Kanaka-landers now had nothing—except for makal, of which there was an abundance. There was makal filling the shops, lining both sides of the high streets of the cities; the village markets sold makal; makal was in the village grocer's shop. The whole country was covered with makal. What was to be done?

Eating the guavas fortified by knowledge proved to be a blessing for the Kanaka-landers. Having consumed the guavas, it did not take them long to think of a way out. They vowed that they would not accept makal anymore. Men, women and children all swore that they were not to be swayed by the magic of makal. This new enthusiasm, the energy that now filled them, would not have been theirs so soon, had they not been drained by makal to this extent. For this they gratefully blessed the djinns many times.

Meanwhile the djinn merchants, as was customary, arrived at the port with shiploads of makal. But this time their makal remained unsold. Since the traders had completely failed at trading, heaps and heaps of beautiful makal kept rotting. Seeing no way out, they sent the news of this misfortune to Paristhan.

Great agitation erupted in the merchant councils of Paristhan on this issue. The waves generated by the controversy shook even the calm waters of the ocean. In the end a toothless, white-haired old man said, 'Investigate and find out why the Kanaka-landers have become disgusted with makal.'

The traders wandered all over Kanakadwipa, listened to various opinions, and learnt that the opponents of makal were those who had tasted guavas. The traders swiftly used their magic and sent this finding to Paristhan. The leader of Paristhan ordered that very day, 'Uproot Kanaka's guava tree.'

Again the traders, with their magic courier, apprised their ruler, 'Impossible to uproot this huge tree. What else do you suggest?'

The leader instantly ordered, 'Cut its roots off.'

The roots of the guava tree were attacked by hundreds of sharp axes. At first, the Kanaka-landers stood stunned at the sight; then they understood what was happening. They tried to dissuade the djinn traders from cutting down the tree by protesting and then pleading with them, falling down weeping at the feet of the merchants. But the djinns did not desist. There followed great disturbance now in Kanakadwipa. The peaceful land was torn from end to end by the fires of unrest. The djinns were, however, relentless. Instead, they tried to bestow their opinion on the golden-bodied people.

'God almighty himself forbade the knowledge fruit for mankind. Moreover, our first mother was expelled from heaven for eating this fruit. You must believe that it is extremely harmful for man. We are working so hard to cut down this tree only as the greatest favour for all of you.'

The people of Kanakadwipa, though, had become sufficiently wise and intelligent and were no longer fooled by empty arguments. They answered with a question: Then why do you eat this fruit? Go and cut down the guava tree in Paristhan and then come and cut our tree. The value of this fruit is easily proved by the fact that our first mother forsook heavenly bliss in return for it. A fruit derived from heaven deserves to be cherished with utter care on earth.

This was the deepest cut of them all. But was anyone listening?

For some time, there was great upheaval in Kanaka over the cutting down of the tree. An octogenarian finally said to his fellow Kanaka-landers, 'Why are you fighting over this gnarled guava tree? This is only a transformed version of that original knowledge fruit. Go and search for the original tree planted by Hava. The holy books say it exists in the eastern part of the world. Come, let us go and find that tree.'

Obeying the old man's advice, everyone

began retracing the road to the past, abandoning the present. However, the old scholar didn't accompany them. He was content with giving them advice.

After travelling for many days, crossing rivers and brooks, cities, mountains, valleys and forests, the Kanaka-landers arrived at last at a spot where a massive dead tree lay prone. Having consulted many ancient literary texts and after hearing countless legends, they concluded that this dead tree was the original tree of knowledge. Their hearts were now pierced by great regret, sorrow and despair. Was it for this dead tree that they had worked so hard, lived exiled from home for many days without food or sleep, suffering so much to come to this region? The inhabitants of this eastern part of the world informed them that the tree died about two hundred years ago. Hearing this, one of the new arrivals commented, 'What a mercy that you have so compassionately spared this tree from becoming fuel. Thank heavens!'

What was to be done now? How could the knowledge tree be brought back to life?

Somebody suggested, 'Let all of us make an effort and pour water at its roots.' Someone said, 'Let us shower it with tears,' and another suggested, 'Let us pour our heart's blood.' Numerous proposals arose of this nature. The Kanaka-landers were prepared to sacrifice even a few human lives if the tree could be revived.

They began lavishing care in all sorts of ways to the dead tree, not sparing even tears or blood. But how can you rejuvenate the dead? Heartbroken to find that their efforts and exertions had failed, the Kanaka-landers began wailing. Exhausted by weeping, one of them lay down under the dead tree.

As he dozed, he dreamt of a sanyasi who said, 'Son, weeping is not going to yield anything. Even if you sacrifice two lakhs of human lives instead of one or two, it is not going to reincarnate the tree of knowledge. Two hundred years ago, some scholar-fools without foresight forbade women to eat the fruit of the knowledge tree. In time that injunction turned into a social convention, and men made the eating of this fruit into a monopoly for themselves. Forbidden from either plucking or tasting this fruit, women ceased to take care of the tree. The knowledge tree thus died, deprived of the tender care of women's hands over many years.

'Go now. Return to your own land. Plant the seed of the guava tree. Let the djinns cut down whichever tree they want. Instead of dissuading them, collect the seeds secretly. If now men and women together nurture the newly-planted seedling, your hopes will be realised.

'Beware! Do not deprive women of guavas. Remember always that women have complete rights over the fruit that once was brought to this realm by a woman!'

On waking from his sleep, the man informed his companions about the dream. On hearing this, everyone agreed to return. A gentleman insightfully asserted, 'Justice indeed! This has been like cheating the crocodile after crossing the river on its back. We were punished adequately for depriving women of knowledge acquired by women.'

Enterprising boys of Kanakadwipa selected and cleared out a corner in a garden, and then called out to the girls, 'Come, sisters. Come and join us. We will prepare the ground with shovels. You plant the seeds. This is an auspicious day. Now we will have our own tree.'

Astounded, the djinns stood and watched silently. They were unable to prevent the Kanaka-landers from executing this promising work. Neither the djinns nor the demons could now obstruct the enthusiastic and inspired Kanaka-landers from their noble objective.

Thereafter, Kanakadwipa once again burst forth with wealth and harvest; the inhabitants lived happily. They were not going to fall for any kind of magic now! For women were now enshrined inside the garden of knowledge.

The legend of Kanaka is nectar-like.
The dead if they hear, will come to life.

NOTES

1. Rokeya's note: This work does not follow the course of events as described in the Quran Sharif or the Bible.

2. Makal: colocynth, a kind of cucumber.

3. Djinn: male. Pari: female.

4. Rokeya's note:

    'Alas! You gave food away
    And received famine in exchange'

SUGRIHINI

The Ideal Housewife (1905)

This is a most important matter. A child's learning occurs simultaneously with its nurture. A doctor once commented, 'Learning how to take care of a child is necessary before one becomes a mother. No one should become a mother without knowing about a mother's responsibilities…' When will a poor girl learn the duties of a mother if she becomes a mother at the age of thirteen, a grandmother when she is twenty-six and a great grandmother at the age of forty?

A child inherits the mother's illnesses, faults, virtues, culture, everything. All great people who are famous in history were children of noble mothers. Sometimes good mothers have bad sons, or good sons are born of bad mothers. These are due to some special circumstances. Generally, it is seen that a custard apple tree will bear custard apples, not jamun. A child loves its mother most, believes in her implicitly. The child will imitate its mother's every act, every word. With every drop of its mother's milk the child absorbs the mother's innermost thoughts. A poet has expressed this so aptly:

...when feeding your child,
O mother, sing then in its ears,
Tales of warriors, of their valour
Let vigour hum in its veins.

Truly, only a brave woman can become the mother of a warrior. If a mother wishes to do so, she can preserve gently all the instincts of a child's heart and build him to be spirited, courageous, brave, steady. Many mothers encourage their children to tell lies and hide the truth. In the future, such boys turn out to be cheats and gamblers.

An incompetent mother will destroy the spirit of her child by beating him for little or no reason. These children turn out to be the ones who will bear, without complaint, a white man throttling them and kicking them with his booted foot. Once, a white man broke his new shoes on the back of a coolie. Relieved that he was not fined for the price of those shoes, the coolie praised the sahib, saying.

'He beat me with new shoes and didn't even charge me for it.' Needless to say, such situations befall many bhadraloks too. Therefore, to bring up a child, both education and intelligence are needed, since the mother is our first, main and natural teacher.

To gain a healthy, strong son, the mother's health must improve. It is indeed very difficult to spend sixteen, seventeen hours just on housework. One needs intervals of rest. Is it not better to spend that time in innocent pastimes rather than in idly gossiping about others or in playing cards? Art and music lessons are useful. She who wishes to be skilful in this will need to be literate. Instructions about colours, brushes, musical notes are to be found in the pages of a book. It is also preferable to utilise your spare hours in reading interesting books and writing poetry.

A few words need to be said regarding the housewife's responsibilities towards her neighbours. Once, the Arabs were famed for hospitality and kindness towards their neighbours. It is said that when an Arab householder was plagued by rats, a friend advised him to keep a cat; however, the man declined, for fear that the rats chased from his house would trouble his neighbour.

We are preoccupied by our concern for our own comfort. Thoughts about the problems of others do not occur to us. Instead, what matters to us first is whether we can gain something from the misfortune of others. If at a time of distress someone is forced to sell his possessions, the buyer is tempted by the possibility of availing an affordable deal. For educated people it is unworthy to be immersed in such small, self-serving matters. For instance, if a good maid is sacked by her mistress out of annoyance, her neighbour instantly tries to grab the worker. The ideal housewife should try to send the maid back to her employer. Regard your neighbour's problems as your own.

Further, the concept of who your neighbours are needs to be expanded. It should not denote just one who lives next doors. Punjab, Ajodhya, Orissa: these are the neighbours of Bengal. A situation may arise, for example, regarding some people who work in a factory in Punjab. Repeated attempts to apprise the factory owners about a problem having failed, the workers take recourse to strike. Let not the people of Madras or Orissa take delight in this, regarding that situation as opportunities for jobs. An ideal housewife should dissuade her husband or son from accepting work where the strike is taking place.

We must remember that we are not merely Hindu, Muslim, Parsi or Christian, nor are we only Bengali, Madrasi, Marwari and Punjabi. We are Indians. We are first Indians—and only then Muslim, Sikh or anything else. The ideal housewife must inculcate this truth in her family. Then, from her home, selfishness, jealousy, envy will be eradicated. Her home will then be as free and compassionate as a holy place. Is there an Indian woman who would not want her home to be like a temple?

(Excerpted from 'Sishu Palon'
(Child care), pages 43-45)

CHASHAR DUKKHU

The Peasant's Sorrow (1920)

I scorch to death in fields, O brother,
Without a rag to cover my bottom.
My wife sold off her bangles,
Yet my kid gets nary a kernel.

I am told that a hundred and fifty years ago, Indians were uncivilised barbarians. But in the hundred and fifty years since then we have become more and more civilised. We are now equal to other countries of the world when it comes to education and access to resources. Now, our civilisation and wealth cannot be contained. Truly, these five-storey-high skyscrapers, railways, tramways, steamers, aeroplanes, lorries, telephones, telegraphs, post offices, regular delivery of letters, a jute mill here, a hessian factory there, clock towers on palatial buildings, eight to ten doctors to check my pulse for a mild malady, medical services, medicines, operations, injections, profusion of arrangements, theatres, bioscopes, the crowds at the races, lemonades, gingerades, ice carts, electric lights, and fans, the sprawl of the honourables, increase of scientific adulterants in foodstuffs—are these not signs of civilisation? Without a doubt! Anyone who denies this is an outright traitor.[1]

But there is another side to things. Calcutta by itself does not comprise the totality of India, and a few fortunate wealthy people do not represent all inhabitants of India. Today, the subject of our discussion is the poverty of peasants. Peasants are the backbone of our society. So why then am I indulging in this rigmarole? There is a reason for this. If I had begun by weeping over the suffering of our village peasants, somebody would quickly prise my eyes open to show me that we now possess cars, gramophones etc. Why focus on the negatives and ignore the positives? So, I put forward all the positive things at the outset. Now let us glance at the downside.

Those jute mills and hessian factories: each worker in a jute mill lives like a nawab and behaves like a nawab on wages of five hundred or seven hundred rupees. But when it comes to the people who produce that jute? The worker there has 'not a rag to cover his bottom.' Should we not think about this? How can Allah-tala tolerate such injustice?

Putting all of India aside, it will be sufficient to discuss only Bengal. If you check only one grain, it should tell you about the cooking of a potful of rice. Our Bengal is well-watered, fertile, green with crops—but why is the peasant's belly empty? Our revered Rabindranath Thakur has answered, 'Rice belongs to the one who owns the land.' True indeed. Who is this luckless peasant? He has to only 'scorch to death on fields', carry the plough, and produce jute. Then what is the purpose of saying that in the peasant's home 'there was a granary full of rice, sheds full of cows, courtyards full of hens'? Does that exist only in the poet's imagination? No. This was not the fancy of a poet, nor some literary text; this was our truth. All this existed in the past, and does not anymore. Arre! Now we are civilised. Is this progress? No use blaming civilisation. The Great European War has impoverished the whole world; why speak of the Bengali peasant?

I cannot be content with the above answer. The European War is a phenomenon only seven years old. Was the peasant's condition better even fifty years ago?

Let me present a few examples. In my childhood, I used to hear that mustard oil sold for eight rupees a seer and ghee for four rupees a seer. Well, here's a story from when mustard oil sold for eight rupees a seer: 'Zamiran the farmer's daughter had thick and long hair. She needed at least a quarter pao² of mustard oil. The day she washed her hair, her mother would bring her to the Raja's house. We would give her oil for her hair.'

What a fate! When oil was available for a few paisas, even then Zamiran's mother couldn't get even a paisa worth of oil.

Just thirty to thirty-five years ago, in Bihar, a peasant wife would sell her daughter for the sake of two seers of kesri dal. Twenty-five years ago, such was the condition in the Kanika district of Orissa that peasants could not afford any garnish except bare salt to eat with their pakhal (stale rice). Dried fish was considered a great delicacy. Rice sold for twenty-five to twenty-six seers for a rupee then. In a village called Sat Bhaya, people couldn't afford even salt to have with their pakhal; they cooked their rice in sea water. Some peasants in the Rongpur district were so poor that they couldn't afford rice, which cost only a rupee for twenty-five seers. They ate boiled pumpkin, gourd or jute greens and gourd leaves. Do you want to know what they wore? With great difficulty, men would procure six or eight hands-width cloth for the women and wore clouts themselves.

During the winters, these men and women would warm themselves by moving around in the fields during the day. At night, if the chill became intolerable, they built fires with jute straw. They slept on beds of straw. Yet this Rongpur is famed for rice and jute. One can see that the European War has very little to do with the poverty of peasants. When twenty-five seers of rice were sold for a rupee, they couldn't fill their bellies: now that three to four seers are available for a rupee, they remain half fasting:

In this cruel world
The peasant is born to suffer.
The pain in his heart is buried,
And hunger burns in his belly.

This was the picture twenty-five to thirty years ago. Which period was it when during which 'there was a granary full of rice, sheds full of cattle, saris of Dacca muslin'? Perhaps that was the condition a hundred years ago.

Then, a peasant woman would spin yarn on the charkha with her own hands and make clothes for the family. In Assam and Rongpur a kind of silk is found which is called 'Endi' in the local language. It is easy to keep Endi insects and make yarn out of their cocoons. This skill was a monopoly of the women of those areas. When they visited each other's homes, they would carry the spindle and keep carding yarn while they strolled. Endi cloth is quite warm and lasts long. It is not inferior to flannel, yet it lasts longer than flannel. A piece of Endi cloth can easily last for up to forty years. If one has four to five pieces of Endi material, there won't be need for quilt, blankets or kanthas made with old saris.

¤

It comes to this, then, that women in the past fulfilled their family's clothing requirements effortlessly. Therefore, the peasant then was not a beggar for food and clothing. But then, he was an uncivilised barbarian. Now he has become civilised, therefore:

He covers his baldness
With a crown

But he gets no rice to fill his belly. One might ask: What is the connection between civilisation and the increase of poverty? The answer: Since brightly-coloured, fine cloth is available at a very affordable price, why bother with the rumble of the charkha? When flannel is available in a variety of colours, why use colourless Endi cloth? Previously, rural women used to make lye at home to wash clothes; now they employ a washerman or buy soda. Why go through the trouble of making lye when the work can be done with four paisa's worth of soda? In this way, wasteful luxury has entered their arteries and veins and poisoned their existence. So now, there may be 'not a rag to cover his bottom', but an umbrella covers the head and shoes are on feet. The wife's gold bangles are sold, but she buys glass bangles. They need coolies and trams to move even a few steps. At first, a five-paisa fare for a tram ride appears insignificant. But, oh dear! A two-way journey ends up costing ten paisas. In this way, losing two paisas here, four paisas there, they've become ruined.

You bartered away your food,
And bought famine in exchange.

Luxury—also known as 'progress'—is accompanied by a new ghost called 'imitation', which sits on their shoulders. As soon as their economic condition improves a little, they start imitating their rich neighbours. The peasant women now need to travel in hired vehicles; they need a labourer to pound their rice. There are so many instances:

The whole body aches: Where do I apply the balm?

Also,

This fire has a hundred flames, who can count
them all?

Ultimately, once the litter-bearers begin travelling around in trams, we will have reached the height of progress.

Notice another interesting phenomenon. Having become completely civilised, we discarded Endi cloth. But Endi became known as 'Assam silk' and turned into coats, pants and skirts, to be seen on the graceful persons of European women. In time, rural women became so civilised that they ceased producing Endi silk. And Assam silk was no longer available in Whiteway Laidlaw. Moreover, now Endi cocoons are sent to England and then reimported as silk yarn.

Recently Lord Carmichael, the Governor of Bengal, was searching for an indigenous silk scarf. No one could inform him where such scarves may be found. But Lord Carmichael is an Englishman, who would not give up so easily; eventually, he discovered the birthplace of that desi scarf. In the past, such silk scarves used to be made in Murshidabad. Now that the people have become civilised, these are no longer woven. The main point here is that as progress advanced, all native industries declined.

Fortunately, the distress in the countryside has attracted the attention of our patriotic leaders. But it is not enough for them to just observe. They have to make special efforts to reduce the suffering of the peasants. The only way to regain that 'granary full of rice, Dacca muslin' is to revive native industries—especially women's industries. In every district, jute cultivation should be reduced and instead cotton grown in large quantities. Also, the promotion of the use of charkha and Endi yarn is desirable. If the women of Assam and Rongpur become active in cultivating Endi insects, the clothing problem of all of Bengal will be solved. Education must be spread in the villages. If there is a school in every village and charkhas and spindles in every home, the poverty of the peasants will end.

NOTES

1. Rokeya's note: In the opinion of many experts, the salt of Liverpool is 'haram'. A person who has tasted the salt of Liverpool and yet refuses to praise the virtues of modern civilisation, is decidedly a 'namakharam' (haram = sin; namakharam = traitor).

2. Pao: a quarter of a seer

SHRISTI TOTWO

The Essence of Creation (1921)

The other day, we were chatting till late at night. We were discussing djinns, paris (fairies), and ghosts. Someone claimed to have seen a white-bearded djinn at namaz, another had seen a fairy in a white dress and one had seen a ghost eating fried fish. Miss Nonibala Dutta fell asleep; I kept sitting on the sofa. Zahida Begum asked me to go to sleep, switched off the lamp and went off to her room. Shireen Begum lay down next to me instead of going to her room. Even without the lamp, the room was quite visible by the light of the candle in the corner. I can't say if I dozed off or not, but I believe I was awake. A few minutes later there was a terrible sound. Nonibala (Noni) startled awake, and asked, 'What is that noise?'

'I can't say. A few days ago, I saw a picture in a newspaper of an aeroplane with a damaged engine falling on the roof of a house. The passenger, completely unhurt, dropped onto the bed inside the room through the hole in the roof. What if some plane has dropped on our worm-eaten roof? Why don't you open the window and check?'

As usual, Binapani Ghosh was fast asleep on her bed. I woke her, saying, 'Out of your bed. Hurry.'

Before my words were out she stumbled out of her bed asking, 'What is the matter?'

I repeated what I'd said to Noni. Noni demurred, 'How can I open the window in all this heavy rain? Besides, I am scared. All those ghost stories you have been telling.'

'All right. I'll open the window,' said Binapani, and unlatched the shutters.

As soon as the window was opened, a gust of wind and rainwater soaked all of us, accompanied by a huge, flaming meteor, which fell into the room. The sight transfixed us. The noise had woken Shireen and Afsar Dulhan, who rushed in from her room and was struck dumb. Unable to decide if we should awaken the household with our screams or escape swiftly, we kept staring with shocked eyes at the fiery pile.

The burning sphere transformed into an incandescent figure. I felt as though I had seen this supernatural being somewhere else, but couldn't identify him properly. It is not my habit to remember people's faces, which gets me into trouble often.

Our fiery visitor spoke up then, and said, 'Girls! You've got a big fright. Let me assure you there is no cause for fear.'

Shireen: The other day a spy came here in the guise of a dumb fakir. Are you one of them?

Noni: You people have taken a house near the Maulana's residence. That is why you are being bothered by these informers.

Fiery figure (forcefully): No, my dear! I am not anyone like that. I am Twosti, the creator of the world.

Upon hearing the name Twosti, Bina and Noni prostrated themselves at his feet.

It was then that I remembered that I had been blessed with a vision of this great spirit, this shape of light, while composing 'Narishristi'. Reverently, we requested Twosti to seat himself.

Bina spoke: May we know the reason why, unseasonably, you have stepped on the dust of this earth? ('Mud' is what one should really say in this rainy season.)

Twosti (pointing at me): This girl is the cause.

Surprised and fearful, I enquired humbly, 'I, my lord? What is this you are saying?'

Twosti: Yes. You. Your Bengali translation of my account of the creation of woman has created a huge furore. Well, why should I blame you? Part of the blame goes to the office of *Saugat*.

Noni: How is that, sir?

Twosti: Well, she had submitted her 'Narishristi' to the *Saugat* monthly magazine. The editor was absent then from Calcutta. The illiterate fellows in the office published the article without two of her footnotes. Without the footnotes, the article was incomprehensible. Intelligent readers felt discontented. Then they declared, 'Call that Twosti. Let him come and explain these lacunae in this article.' So, whenever they feel like it, they call me by planchette and drag me from heaven to bother me.

Listen to what happened today. Some young men here have got tremendously excited by the Satyagraha movement. Our rulers say, 'Abandon Satyagraha, adopt Mithyagraha.' But these simple youngsters won't listen to such kind suggestions. Two lawyers, who wouldn't accept Mithyagraha, were chased by the police and have escaped to Ranchi. Their house is quite close to your residence.

But you know that 'the devil doesn't listen to scriptures.' They refuse to be at peace even in all this rain and mud of Ranchi.

Covered from top to toe in sand, gravel, mud, and water—all afternoon long, they disturb the peace of the countryside, leaving no stone unturned to preach against Mithyagraha and expose the truth.

Even at night the two friends shake up the peace of the abode of the gods. From 12pm to 1pm, we have to be on our toes since these lawyers keep calling us up.

On earth, at least you have the CID to punish these young spoilers of peace. But in heaven we have no provision for keeping them in check!

That is how, late at night, on my way back from the lawyer's home, my steam vehicle got entangled with the dome of your house. My fall was noisy but I survived. Can't stand getting wet at my age. So as soon as brave Bina opened the window, I entered your room.

Noni: But lord! Our window has iron bars!

Twosti: Arre! Forget your worm-eaten bars! Besides, who can stop me!

Noni: Lord, we are very curious to learn what elements you used to create man.

Twosti: No, my child. I have no time now. Let me leave. Go to sleep.

But all of us prevailed upon him strongly to stay. We were determined to not let him leave before he revealed the mystery of the creation of man.

Shireen: You've stayed soaked from the rain for a long time. Would you like a cup of tea? Begin your account, sir. I'll just order tea. Maro![1]

Twosti (gives a start): Who is she going to beat?

Shireen hid her laughter with the end of her sari and left quickly.

Twosti: Did she leave to call a guard?

Bina (trying not to laugh): No. She left to call her maid. The girl is called Maro. Please begin your story now. Look, Shireen is back.[2]

Twosti: Since you are not going to spare me, what can I do? I see that you women are as tough as these lawyers. They at least have laws and statutes in their favour. But you do not observe even that. But what will you learn if you only listen? So, Noni, go fetch some paper and a pen. You must write down quickly as I describe. Now, you must write fast.

While Noni went to find the paper and pen, Bina advanced with paper and a pencil and said, 'Lord, don't worry about time being short. Speak and I'll take it down in shorthand. I can take down three hundred words a minute in shorthand.' Lord Twosti was very pleased to hear this. So he spoke, Bina wrote, and we listened.

I could see poor Twosti-dev felt very sleepy. Sometimes he yawned and, drowsy-eyed, spoke softly; then, suddenly, he would rub his eyes, speak up loudly and check Bina's writing. If he found a mistake he would make her write again. All this was to show that he was not sleepy.

At one point he roared, 'You know, girls? At the time of creating women, I had nothing left in my hands. Therefore, I had to collect the fragrance from some things, the taste from some things and just vapour from some element.

'But I didn't have to worry while creating man. I had everything available in large quantities in my store. Effortlessly I reached out and picked up whatever fell into my hands. For instance, to fashion their teeth I used the serpent's fangs in entirety; hands, feet, nails were made out of all the claws of the tiger. To complete the cells of the brain, I used up the brains of the donkey. To create women, I used up the warmth of the fire, but for men I used the burning coal itself. Now child, do write all this down.'

Bina wrote: 'Burning coal.'

Twosti: Now girls, listen carefully. For women I used only the coolness of snow, for men whole pieces of ice. I even made use of the entire Kanchenjunga Mountain. Have you written that, Bina?

Bina showed her paper, where she had written: 'Ice, Kanchenjunga.'

Shireen: It is doubtless that Vesuvius and Kanchenjunga have been placed next to each other within the male. This is confirmed in the words of men themselves, described in this manner:

> *One moment*
> *From his forehead arose pointed flames,*
> *Fire flooded that barren countryside,*
> *Byomkesh Rudra assumed his destructive aspect.*
> *With a roar he grabbed his death spear*
>
> *And the next moment,*
> *At Parvati's appeal, abandoning his aggression,*
> *Smiling he addressed Indra,*
> *'It will be unjust of me to slay Britro.'*

The dictation being over, Twosti said, 'Listen child. When you transcribe this in normal language, be very careful. Not a single word or full stop must be misplaced.'

Bina: I'll do that. Please don't worry. I will write with great care. Or else you, prabhu, may suffer greatly. At the moment it is men who keep calling you up. Women might also begin to trouble you.

Finally, Twosti having departed, we took to our beds. Somehow, as I began to lie down, I fell. The fall shocked me. Opening my eyes, I found myself still sitting on the sofa, the candle burning in the corner, Shireen and Bina sleeping the sleep of the dead. Faraway, the cock crowed. The night had ended.

Had I been dreaming all this while?

NOTES

1. Maro in Bengali means 'beat, assault'.

2. Rokeya's note: The poor maid's beautiful name 'Mariam' has turned into the nickname 'Maro'. While living in Bihar, I had the good fortune to meet some wellborn women called 'Hasho', 'Lato', 'Dalloo', 'Ullu', and 'Jubba'. Unfair to not give their real names, or readers may be scared like Twosti: Hashmat Ara, Latifunnesa, Daulatunnesa, Alimunnesa, Zubeida!

THE APPEAL

(Poem, 1921)

We the landowners
And all titleholders,
Property owners from Bengal and Bihar,
Fervently we appeal all together.
Better to lose our lives,
And die a thousand times
Than bear to be parted from our tails.

From Bombay it hails,
Bharat Somoy[1] it is named
The white man's paper, fury-filled,
'Catch these mute men,
Cut off their tails,
Most proper punishment for them.'[2]

'No foe has a dumb man.'
In this truth we believed.
Bearers of tails, silent we stayed.
Out of a cloudless sky,
Sudden thunder we hear!
Our tails will be severed!
All for speaking not a word!

Where lives this barbarian,
One who preaches 'sedition'?
Let the thunder fall on his head!
Now cease, you rebels,
Waste not your precious breath,
Pen, and tongue on 'Swaraj.'

Raise voices, O fellow travellers,
To the highest decibel.
Announce for all to know,
We never broke the Law.

Signatures:
Landowners, Tail bearers, Zamindars,
All famished and civilised ones.

(First published in *Sadhana*, 1921)

NOTES

1. *The Times of India.*

2. 'Moderates who are keeping silence, who ought to be deprived of their titles.'

NIRUPAM BIR

Incomparable Warrior (Poem, 1922)

The Judge says, 'Kanai, now you will hang.'
Kanai smiles his scorn.
For those who made a life from sacrifice,
The noose is no terror
And death is a trifle.

Incomparable Kanai,
His glory is without question.
Destined to die Kanai,
Soon to be immortal,
Who can ever erase him?
Flesh and blood Kanai,
A body once tied
To this earthly realm.
Forever free Kanai
Walking from his cage

To become a million Shyams,
Spread from horizon to horizon of this land.
(All hail his name)

The people of Bengal
Prayed in his name
And many bowed at his prison gate.
In the world beyond, no praise for Kanai,
Though reverence flows like a river
Through the hearts of Bengal.
Though it may be lost in the outer world,
In the Indian heart a flame burns eternal,
And all the brave on waking
Have only one name to greet the morn.

So, say, say now, 'Vande Shyam.'

(First published in *Dhumketu*, 1922)

RANI BHIKARINI

The Beggar Queen (1927)

Miss Mayo, the American writer, has drawn a very striking picture of the sufferings of Hindu women in her book *Mother India*. The Hindus may curse Miss Mayo to their heart's content for stating the brutal truth, but the violence of their abuses will not transform a black crow into a white duck. Illegitimate and abandoned infants will not come back to life, various ailments afflicting a twelve-year-old pregnant mother will not be healed, and nor will the number of female patients in hospitals reduce. Indian leaders say *Mother India* has focused only on negative aspects of Indian culture, and no mention has been made of the country's excellences. However, the point is that what is good is already perfect and does not need to change. It is essential to reform that which is wrong.

When a doctor conducts a health check-up, he concentrates on the patient's illnesses and prescribes medicines. When a doctor checks your eyesight, he prescribes spectacles instead of giving you a certificate of merit for your digestive system. Approximately sixteen crores of Indian men exist to sing praises of India's perfections. Do you need a Miss Mayo to beat on that triumphant drum? A Miss Mayo is needed to state that which no one has ever uttered till now, that which no one has dared to mention. This is the same truth that I have been stressing for the last twenty years. But no one heard my faint voice. Miss Mayo's roar has drawn everyone's attention.

The father figures of India are engaged in a bitter fist fight with the author of *Mother India*. Muslims, seize the moment to see your image in this mirror. Look at how in your community you have turned a queen into a beggar. No country, race or religion has ever given any rights to women in this entire world. Even the possession of souls has been denied to women. Islam alone has given women rights which belong to them. But in India, the suffering of the Muslim woman has reached the nadir.

Where no society has ever given property

rights to daughters, Islam alone has allowed daughters a share equal to their brothers' in their father's property. Wives in other communities cannot retain their property. Whatever money a wife brings from her father's home passes into her husband's control. The wife is allowed no use of it. A Muslim wife, however, has the right to enjoy her own wealth freely. Furthermore, at the time of her marriage, she is endowed with whatever money or wealth her husband can afford, on account of 'den-mohar'. On the death of her husband, there is provision for the wife to claim her 'den-mohar' and, even before the division of the property among the children and other heirs, claim one-eighth of the property that is due to her by right. What remains after the wife's share is distributed amongst the rest.

Hinduism prescribes for its widow death by burning along with her husband. The condition of present-day widows is more death than life. Cartloads of Hindu shastras lay down that 'it is not enough for a widow to abstain from marrying a second time. A widow should give up all kinds of pleasurable foods and survive merely on fruits and herbs.' Islam, however, has permitted widows to remarry, and widows are not oppressed in any manner. There are no restrictions with regard to a widow's clothing, ornaments and food.

Hindus are obliged by their shastras to treat a wife on par with a domestic animal or a slave. Marrying a daughter off at the age of eight brings them the merit of having performed 'gouri-dan'. Under Islamic faith, however, women have been granted full independence. It has been declared that 'heaven is to be found at the feet of a mother'. No woman can be married without her consent. This has indirectly prevented child marriages.

According to Hindu shastras, 'if a woman is educated she will become a widow.'

Our Rasul-Allah has said, 'Talabul ilmi farizatun, ala kutli Muslimeen wa Muslimatun.' That is, it is the duty of all Muslim men and women to be educated equally.

But what is it that we see in reality? The Hindus have enacted laws to enable their daughters to inherit property. They have the right to execute wills. They can will away all their wealth to a wife or a daughter, whereas Muslims deprive their daughters of their share in the property by making them sign 'no claims to property'. In many heinous ways, women are deprived of a share in their father's or husband's property.

The Hindus are trying their utmost to establish widow remarriage. Our so-called Ashrafs instead derive great honour by keeping their seven-year-old widowed daughters as lifelong widows.

The Hindus are promulgating laws to prevent child marriages. The minimum age at which girls will be legally allowed to marry will be set at sixteen (though pundits are loudly proclaiming them as 'non–Hindus' for this). What do I find in our community? A minor, a nine-year-old child is being married to a groom living in a faraway land with the help of the telegraph. Often, a girl who is a major may cry her heart out, soaking with tears her clothes because her marriage has been fixed with some sixty-year-old man or a drunkard of dubious reputation. The wedding ceremony is concluded while these tears of heartbreak continue to fall. The bride refuses to say yes, but her inflexible guardians execute the marriage by eventually forcing assent out of her mouth.

Now Hindus are granting freedom to women with great generosity. Sons and daughters are being educated equally. Hindu girls are now passing out of Sanskrit tols,[1] village schools and high schools to conquer the university. Yet our community refuses to let us glimpse the light of education.

Around sixty to seventy years ago, English education was forbidden even for men. People were declared kafirs for studying English. Now, the leaders of our community are reaping the fruits of that. Health, finance, the armed forces, power, education: all these departments are barred for Mussalmans, the reason cited being their incompetence. For the sake of getting fifty percent of the jobs in the Calcutta Corporation, Mussalmans have shouted themselves hoarse to enter the list of India's most depressed class.

Here, I too have to say that their incompetence is very real. Whether Mussalmans agree or not, there is not an iota of doubt that they are incompetent. It is only natural that compared to the children of educated, efficient mothers, children of illiterate, inefficient mothers like the Mussalmans will be inferior. Instead of becoming angry at being called 'incompetent', it is far better to try and become competent.

NOTE

1.   Tol: A special school for Sanskrit education in Bengal.

SUBAH SADEK

True Dawn (1931)

Awake, mothers! Sisters! Daughters!

Rise. Abandon your beds. Advance! Listen. The muezzin sounds the azan. Can you not hear Allah's call, the azan? Sleep no more. Rise. Now the night has passed. It is now true dawn. The muezzin has called the azan.

All over the world women have awakened. They have called out against various social evils. They have become ministers of education, doctors, philosophers, scientists, and ministers of war, chief of the army, writers, and poets. But we, the women of Bengal, are fast asleep on the dark and dank floors inside the prisons of our homes, dying of consumption in thousands.

We have reserved all sorts of curses for ourselves by resolving not to step in concert with the march of time. We have vowed not to heed the call of the azan. Sisters, just peep out of the tiny holes in your own prisons and glance at the world outside.

From the moment of our birth we have heard that we are slaves, eternal slaves and will remain slaves.

Ah! How sadly the poet sang:

I cannot express the pain in my heart.
How heavy were my sins that I am a woman?

Accusing us as 'Na ke sul aql',[1] all the evil in the world is piled on our shoulders. We have been mute and have never protested against these unfair judgements. We feel gratified at being treated like animals.

Recently, our masters have begun valuing us as jewels. Look at how many 'Defence of Women' societies are being established! Truly, since we are no better than living luggage, alert guards are needed to prevent us from being abducted.

My unfortunate sisters, does it not make you feel ashamed? If it does, why do you silently swallow this insult?

Take a look at yourselves. We are considered equivalent to animals. So, see, side-by-side with 'Society for Prevention of Cruelty to Animals' is situated 'The Committee for the Defence of Women'. Can there be an insult worse than this? These insults must now end.

Sisters! Rub sleep out of your eyes. Walk forward. Be brave! Say, Ma, 'We are not animals!' Say, sisters, 'We are not furniture!' Say, daughters, 'We are not meant to be buried inside iron chests as bejewelled ornaments!'

In one voice declare, 'We are human!' Show actively that we are half of the best part of creation. In reality, it is we who are the mothers of the created world.

Form your own associations yourselves to defend your own rights and demands.

The infallible remedy needed to prevent all kinds of injustices is the spread of education. At the least, girls must be given primary education. By education I have in mind 'positive training'. To be able to read a few books or write a few verses does not amount to real education.

The education I want is that which will enable them to acquire citizen's rights, which will make them into ideal daughters, sisters, housewives and ideal mothers.

Education must cater to both the mind and the body. Women must know that they have been born into this world not to become playthings dressed in beautiful saris, hair clips, and expensive ornaments. Instead, they have been born as women to fulfil a particular responsibility. Their lives are not to be dedicated to please their husbands like gods. Let them not be at the mercy of anyone for food and shelter.

In my opinion, for physical training, learning the skill of fighting with sticks and knives, learning to husk rice by dheki, grinding wheat and performing all household chores is best. Husking rice and grinding wheat may additionally help solve the great food problem in the country. Presently, for want of husked rice and ground wheat, death is carrying people away as if in a flood. Instead of jumping around or dancing, this kind of bodily culture is a hundred times preferable. Walks in the morning are also desirable.

The government is now concentrating on the care of children. That is excellent. But first, it is necessary to strengthen the mother of the children.

Whatever happens, mothers, sisters, daughters! Sleep no more. Arise and proceed towards your responsibilities.

NOTE

1. Na ke sul aql (Arabic) probably means 'without brains'.

NARIR ODHIKAR

The Rights of Women (1932)

In our religion, a marriage is completed only after the bride and groom have both consented. If, by mischance (let Khoda prevent it), it should come to divorce, it should happen by the consent of both. But why then, in practice, is divorce always one-sided, initiated only by the husband? At least this is what we see every time. In our North Bengal, I have seen talaq is very common amongst the middle classes. That is, the husband abandons his wife on the smallest of pretexts. If there is the smallest mistake by the woman, the man goes around arrogantly proclaiming, 'I am going to give her talaq today.' Then some women sit inside a room surrounding that luckless girl; on the veranda or courtyard sit some men with that creature called her husband. In the presence of these men the husband announces loudly, three times:

Ayen talaq, bayen talaq,
Talaq, talaq, tin talaq
Today I give my joru talaq.

The man looks very cheerful at this time. Most probably joyful in expectation of a new bride. But the girl cries very hard. Then some senior lady takes off the ornaments from her nose, ears and wrists, and ties them up in the end of her sari. The glass bangles on her wrists are broken with a piece of brick or wood, and she is told, 'Forfeit your den-mohar before you leave.' The girl cries even more. Poor girl, having lost her husband, her ornaments, her precious home built by her own hands, cries at her own deprivation.

The next scene: the man goes off on a vacation with his cronies. And the father, brother, uncle or whoever is present as the guardian of the girl (one or two such people are fetched beforehand), that supposed guardian of the still weeping girl drags her with force into a palki and leaves.

In North Bengal there is a poem about the eagerness and desire of old men to marry nubile young women:

Hukur, hukur, coughs the old man,
Hukur, hukur, he coughs.
Nikah makes the old man laugh,
Fukur, fukur he laughs.

ROKEYA SAKHAWAT HOSSAIN

Life and Letters

Rokeya Sakhawat Hossain was born in 1880 in Pairaband village in the Northern District of Rongpur in East Bengal. The Saber clan to which she belonged descended from an Iranian elite who had travelled from Tabriz in Iran to make his fortune under the Mughals. For his services to the Emperor and the Nawab, Tabrizi was awarded a large landholding free of tax in Rongpur, Bengal.

As time passed, this huge zamindari and its wealth fractured into ever-smaller portions amongst the numerous branches of the clan, and was frittered away mainly due to their spendthrift ways. When Rokeya was born, for her own family there was not much remaining of past prosperity. Her father's four wives and their many children comprised a populous household. Rokeya's father, Zahiruddin Saber, followed his forefathers' luxurious lifestyle, particularly a predilection for engaging in litigations. Towards the end of his life, Zahiruddin suffered complete destitution, reduced to surviving on the charity of his former tenants.

Their noble birth, wealth, and the distinction of foreign lineage created a gulf between the Sabers and their peasant subjects in Pairaband. As was the prevailing custom amongst the Ashrafs, the Muslim elites of Bengal, members of the family were discouraged from speaking in Bengali. The Sabers maintained their aloofness by shunning the Bengali language. Urdu and Persian were cultivated. What is remarkable in this context is that Rokeya attained great proficiency in Bengali and became a prolific writer in many prominent journals.

The prohibition regarding the language spoken at home sometimes led to piquant situations. In 'Lukono Ratan' (A hidden jewel), 1927, Rokeya described an incident concerning her sister, Karimunnessa, the hidden jewel of the title. The child Karimunnessa was once poring over a piece of writing in a disreputable Bengali journal that had fallen into her hands when her father appeared. Contrary to the terrified child's expectations, father Zahiruddin, appreciating the keenness of her desire to read Bengali, arranged for lessons. Even this small concession inflamed the ire of the community elders. So strong was their condemnation that the lessons were discontinued and Karimunnessa was soon married and banished to distant Baliadi, a stronghold of conservatism.

Karimunnessa and Rokeya, however, defiantly maintained their devotion to Bengali. They attained such proficiency in Bengali that they adopted it as the vehicle of their creativity. Karimunnessa was a poet; Rokeya a witty, incisive, polemical journalist and fiction writer. It is worth remembering that many decades later, equally fervent devotion to their mother tongue Bangla led to ferocious agitation in erstwhile East Pakistan and was a factor in the ensuing liberation war, which resulted in the birth of Bangladesh.

The Saber clan observed the strictest form of purdah. Bittersweet reflections of the experience of living under purdah have been captured in Rokeya's vignettes in 'Aborodhbasini', translated as 'In Seclusion' by Roshan Jahan.[19] What is remarkable is that out of such an utterly restrictive environment Rokeya emerged as a person and writer of inflexible personality and convictions. Unflinching support from her elder brother Ibrahim Saber, sister Karimunnessa, and later from her liberal, educated husband Sakhawat Hossain, made this possible.

Rokeya's brothers Ibrahim Saber and Khalilur Saber were the first men of the family to receive a Western education. In that period, Indian Muslims were emerging from the defeated stupor and proud isolation of the post mutiny period. The Saber brothers studied at St Xavier's College in Calcutta. Rokeya's first visit to Calcutta was as her mother's companion on a visit to her brothers. Interestingly, given the political context of the two stories in this volume—of opposition to British rule in India—while in Rongpur, the Saber brothers were associated with Rongpur's civil surgeon Dr K D Ghosh, the father of revolutionary Aurobindo Ghosh.

One of the most evocative stories among many of the various surprising ways in which Indian women in the past acquired knowledge comes from Rokeya's childhood. Appreciating the keen intelligence of his little sister, Ibrahim Saber began instructing her in English, believing that in the future, the language would be the key to all societal progress. Late at night when that vast household fell asleep, by the light of a candle the brother and sister pored over English lessons. Ibrahim ignored the prohibitions regarding language and girls' education that were prevalent in the class and place to which he belonged. Rokeya paid tribute to her brother in the dedication to her novel 'Padmarag', 1922. How successful those surreptitious lessons were can be seen in the fluid language of Rokeya's famous fantasy, 'The Sultana's Dream'. Meanwhile Rokeya's sister Karimunnessa, banished to Baliadi, did not accept defeat but continued her study of Bengali. She shared lessons with her sympathetic brothers-in-law and she encouraged Rokeya to continue her Bengali studies.

At the age of sixteen, Rokeya was married to Syed Sakhawat Hossain, then thirty-six, of Bhagalpur. Sakhawat Hossain was a deputy magistrate in Bihar. He had been a brilliant student and had studied agricultural science in England. The Saber brothers found this educated, cultured civil servant a suitable match for their intelligent young sister, though he was a widower and did not speak Bengali.

With her husband, Rokeya travelled extensively in Bihar and observed the customs and restrictions in the lives of Muslim women. This knowledge helped her as a writer and an activist in the cause of women's rights and furnished the subject of some stories in *Aborodhbasini*.

The marriage was in most ways a fortunate one for Rokeya, as far as the development of her mind and personality is concerned. Sakhawat Hossain encouraged his wife to continue to read and write. It is in this period that Rokeya wrote her utopian satire, 'Sultana's Dream'.

However, it was a very short married life of nine years for Rokeya. Sakhawat Hossain fell seriously ill, and had to be taken to Calcutta. In spite of Rokeya's devoted nursing, he expired in 1909 after suffering for two years. There were no children of the marriage, their two children having died in infancy.

The indulgent Sakhawat Hossain, appreciative of Rokeya's interest in girls' education, had left a sum of ten thousand rupees for her to use. After her husband's death, Rokeya established a school for girls in Bhagalpur. Those were her first steps towards emancipating women's lives through education. However, intrigues by relatives made her life so difficult that in 1910 she moved to Calcutta with her mother. The very next year her mother passed away, leaving Rokeya's position as a single woman vulnerable, exposed to inimical social scrutiny.

With a will of iron, Rokeya threw herself into the project of establishing a school for Muslim girls in her husband's name. There was a great deal of opposition at that time to education for girls of elite families, even more to the idea of a young personable widow engaging in such an enterprise. The principal of a girls' school described how Rokeya quietly sat in the classrooms or in the office to observe first-hand how to run a school for girls. In 1911, with eight students and two benches, Rokeya achieved her dream in a small way.

Urdu was the language of instruction in the school Rokeya esatablished, which had to relocate three times in search for suitable premises. Rokeya was both the headmistress of the institution and secretary of the school board. Many well-known, distinguished personalities of Calcutta were patrons of her school and members of the school committee.

Severe financial crisis made Rokeya's work difficult. She lost a great deal of money when a bank failed. To secure and then increase government aid, Rokeya had to struggle relentlessly. A government grant was of utmost importance for a financially deprived school. Rokeya pleaded for an increase in the amount of aid, since she wanted to raise her school to higher classes and expand the curriculum. Evidence is to be found in her letters and in the many articles where she brings her sharp wit and sarcasm to make passionate appeals to the leaders and influential people of her community to help the cause of women's education.

Additionally, to persuade Muslim families to allow their daughters to acquire education, it was incumbent upon Rokeya to make a strong commitment to purdah. The Sakhawat Memorial Girls School maintained very stringent purdah custom. Yet her critics in the community found faults with the smallest infringement of purdah, such as curtains moving while students were being transported by covered horse-carriage to school.

Rokeya submitted to all these restrictions, though she must have seethed within. She sacrificed her own freedom for the sake of the school. During meetings of the school committee, she, as the secretary, sat behind a curtain, while a Christian member of staff moved with files and papers between the members of the committee and the headmistress. This was a period when all those who worked in the field of girls' education in India, in whichever community, were extremely cautious to vouchsafe strictest adherence to purdah, whether it was the Bethune School in Calcutta or the Indraprastha Girl's School in Delhi.

Rokeya's energy, enthusiasm and determination were inexhaustible. She supervised all aspects of running the school for girls, knowing she could not afford any laxity, given that hostile forces were ranged against her. Rokeya struggled all her life to raise sufficient funds to construct a building for her school. She wrote letters and articles, and spoke at gatherings to persuade influential and affluent people to materially contribute to and actively support her school and alleviate the sufferings in the lives of Muslim women.

However, Rokeya did not confine herself only to the needs of her students. She concerned herself with overall improvement of the lives of women in society. Women's health was one of her abiding interests. Aware of the limits of freedom granted to Muslim women, Rokeya exhorted them to move around in open air, even if in their burkhas, instead of being confined inside the house. Her articles were targeted at men, knowing they held power and control over lives of women. A famous exhortation likened the relationship of men and women in society to two wheels of a carriage which must move in concert if smooth progress was to be achieved.

Rokeya's career as a writer had begun many years prior to her establishing the girls' school. She wrote for many Bengali journals, and had published 'Sultana's Dream' in *The Indian Ladies Journal*. In Calcutta, she came in contact with a lively literary circle. All the important journals solicited her contributions. In this period, she wrote copiously, with literary pieces such as 'Pipasa' (Thirst), 1906, but also articles in which she deplored the downtrodden condition of Indian women and articles where she mocked what she perceived as the weak sterility of Bengali men.

In 1905, a selection of six articles by Rokeya, which had previously appeared in various journals earlier, was published as *Motichur*. This was the first volume. It is the second volume of *Motichur* that contains the two allegorical stories which have been translated here. Rokeya's writing was only an extension of her work as a social reformer, especially her goal of emancipating women from the neglect and contempt of men.

In addition to her unceasing work as a school principal, a writer, and a public speaker on education and women's causes, Rokeya was also a keen observer of the national political scene. In that period, this was largely synonymous with following the activities of the Congress party. The Indian National Congress was born in 1885 in Bombay, just five years after the birth of Rokeya. This fact becomes interesting in the context of 'Muktiphal', one of the fables presented here, written on the occasion of a cataclysmic event in the Congress in 1907: the splitting of the party into two factions, within twenty years of its founding.

Rokeya had strong convictions regarding the struggle for freedom from colonial rule, dictated by her fearless independent spirit. Her nephews, the Guznavi brothers, sons of Karimunnessa, became important leaders of the Congress party in Bengal. One of them was a member of one of the Round Table Conferences in London. Political commitment was part of her family environment.

The story 'Muktiphal' ('The Freedom Tree'), in this book, is her critique of how the men of the

Congress party were slowing down the course of the Independence movement by their lack of unity, objectivity or a concerted plan of action. 'Muktiphal' is a satire in the mode of Jonathan Swift of 18th century England.

The other satire in this book, 'Gyanphal', in the form of rup-katha, or fairy tale, is an allegorical version of how India became colonised. Rokeya began her history with Adam and Eve in the Garden of Eden, proceeding to the story of a once-fabulous Kanakadwipa conquered by the cunning paris (fairies) from a distant land. She adroitly brings together her engagement with the cause of India's freedom and her undeviating agenda of women gaining power through knowledge. In keeping with the theme of other works, Rokeya unequivocally points to the long suppression of women and their deprivation of knowledge as the reason for the downfall of India, i.e. Kanakadwipa.

What is unique to her is that as a writer and activist, Rokeya insisted on relating whatever the topic or theme in hand was to the condition of women. For an activist who has a firmly perceived goal and is aware that the path is not going to be easy, there is no alternative except to be relentless in pursuing it. For Rokeya Sakhawat Hossain that cause was to wrest freedom for women from the oppression of male domination. Education, to her, was the magic formula that would open the minds of women.

She herself was aware of all the issues that featured in public discourse at that time. Whichever subject she may be focussing on as a writer, a speaker, an organiser, her undeviating glance would be fixed on how the predicament and participation of women were implicated there. The fables 'Muktiphal' and 'Gyanphal' are no exceptions to this.

Rokeya founded, in 1916, the first society for Muslim women, Anjuman-i-Khawateen-i-Islam, to create a forum where women could speak freely and become more aware of their condition. It was imperative to her that women of her community developed a consciousness about themselves and the issues which concerned them.

The woman-centric nature of her thought can sometimes surprise us by how far reaching and comprehensive it could be. In the article 'Endi Shilpo' from 1920, she deplores the extinction of Endi-worm cultivation in her part of Bengal. She believed that in the past, in Rongpur, impoverished peasant women cultivated and prepared Endi yarn, which provided a means of subsistence through carding of raw silk. At her own expense she initiated a search for someone in the Bengal countryside who still preserved the skill of weaving Endi yarn. In all of Rongpur she could find only one such person.

Rokeya's active personality and pragmatism soon made her invaluable to many women's organisations active in the country at that time, which were trying to highlight various women's causes. She was associated with most of the famous Indian women leaders of that time. Sarojini Naidu commended Rokeya's work as an educationist in a letter. Bi Amma, Begum of Bhopal, and other radical Muslim reformers were closely associated with Rokeya.

Never having studied in a school or a college, Rokeya became a person who was sought by anyone who required genuine information about the state of Muslim women in Bengal. In 1926, she was invited to give the Presidential address at the Bengal Women's Educational Conference. In her own signature ironic vein, Rokeya expressed her bitter disappointment that, after twenty years of work to advance the cause of education and social improvement in the lives of Muslim women, in all of Bengal she could find only one Muslim woman graduate. Yet, there is a reference in one of her letters to a relative, to her despairing at being unable to complete a graduation degree due to her pressing schedule.

In 1925, she was a special invitee in an Educational Conference in Aligarh. This conference is memorable for the revolt by attending women delegates against docile spectatorship. Atiya Begum from Bombay led the revolt. Rokeya, representing Bengal, spoke fearlessly on injustice against women, undeterred by the presence of powerful male delegates. She had indeed travelled far from the claustrophobic seclusion of Pairaband.

Full as her life was as a writer, a journalist, a feminist activist, and a school secretary, Rokeya's personal life was bleak. A rare expression of a sense of deprivation is found in a letter occasioned by the death of Noori, her niece who she had hoped to adopt. She felt destiny snatched away all those on whom she bestowed affection—her husband, her two infants. Yet bereavement did not dim her zest for her mission, nor render her grim. She responded with joy whenever an occasion for a new experience came her way. In the article

'Bayujane Ponchas Mile' (Fifty miles by airplane), 1931, there is great exhilaration when she enjoyed a flight on an airplane flown by a nephew.

The life of this indefatigable, forceful personality came to an end on the night of 9th December, 1932. It is difficult to miss the symbolic aura in the way she died. Till late at night, Rokeya was dealing with documents concerning her school. In the morning, on that table, under a paperweight were discovered pages of the incomplete manuscript of 'Narir Odhikar' ('The Rights of Women'), an essay on the tragedy of triple talaq (divorce). An existing heart condition had taken away her breath at the very moment she was putting her heart into articulating the motive force of her life's work. She was only fifty-three.

Eighty-four years later we can only appreciate the adamantine nature of the problems against which Rokeya had pitted herself. The topic of those last few paragraphs Rokeya wrote in that unfinished article was the custom of triple talaq (divorce) in the Muslim community. In three paragraphs, Rokeya described how a woman's life could be shattered by the irresponsible utterance of talaq by a husband. She questioned this unequal and unjust custom.

At the moment of writing this, in 2018, Muslim women in India are once again challenging the law by which Muslim men can divorce their wives with the greatest of ease, made worse by availability of electronic devices. The equitable and dignified life for Indian women that Rokeya had envisaged still appears to be a distant dream. What has changed is that women have found a voice to launch a strong movement, in the media and in courts, to have this shameful custom stopped. The confidence in their voices is the gift of pioneering women such as Rokeya Sakhawat Hossain, who fought for women's rights.

LIST OF ROKEYA'S WORKS CITED
IN *FREEDOM FABLES*

Abarodhbasini 1928
Address to Bengal Women's Educational Conference 1926
Amader Abanati 1905
Ardhangi 1905
Bayujane Ponchas Mile 1931
Chashar Dukkhu 1921
Endi Shilpo 1920
Gyanphal 1907, 1921
Interview with Begum Tarzi 1929
Lukono Ratan 1927
Motichur I 1905
Motichur II 1921
Muktiphal 1907 ,1921
Narir Odhikar 1932
Nari Shrishti 1918
Niriho Bangali 1903
Nirupam Bir 1922
Padmarag 1924
Pipasa 1906

Rani Bhikarini 1927
Rasana Puja 1904
Shristi Totwo 1920
Strijatir Abanati 1904
Subah Sadek 1931
Sugrihini 1905
Sultana's Dream 1905
The Appeal 1921

BIBLIOGRAPHY

Dua, R P. *Social Factors in the Birth and Growth of the Indian National Congress Movement with Special Reference to the Period Leading to 1885 till 1935*, S. Chand & Co, Delhi, 1967.

Dutta, P K. 'Abduction in Bengal of 1920s' in *Studies of History*, Jan–Jun 1998, Sage.

Farooqui, Rashid Ali. *Bangla Upanyase Musalman Lekhokder Abadan*, Ratna Prakashan, 1984.

Goswami, Anjan. *Itihaser Prokkhapote Hindu-Musalman*, Chirayata Prakashan Pvt Ltd, Kolkata, 1995.

Hasan, Morshed Shafiul. *Begum Rokeya: Somaj o Sahitya*, Maola Brothers, Dhaka, 1982.

Islam, Sirajul. 'Social and Cultural History' in *History of Bangladesh, 1704–1971*, Asiatic Society of Bangladesh, 1992.

Low, D A. *The Indian National Congress: Centenary Highlights*, Oxford University Press, 1988.

Mahmud, Moshafeqa. *Potre Rokeya Porichiti*, Naya Udyog, 1996.

Mahmud, Shamsun Nahar. *Rokeya Jiboni*, Sahitya Prakashan, 1996.

Maitra, Bhobesh. *Begum Rokeya*, Kolkata 2005.

Morshed, Gholam. *Rassundari Theke Rokeya: Nari Progotir Eksho Bochor*, Bangla Akademi, Dhaka, 1999.

Sarkar, Sumit. *Modern India 1885–1947*, Palgrave Macmillan, 1989.

Sarkar, Sumit, and Tanika Sarkar. *Women and Social Reform in Modern India Vol. II*, Permanent Black, 2007.

Sen, Abhijit. *Ogronthito Rokeya*, Naya Udyog, Kolkata 1998.

Southard, Barbara. *The Women's Movement and Colonial Politics in Bengal: The Question of Political Rights, Education and Social Reform Legislature, 1921–1936*, Manohar, 1995.

Sufi, Motaphar Hosain. *Begum Rokeya; Jibon o Sahitya*, Dhaka, 2001.

Zakaria, Rafiq. *Rise of Muslims in Indian Politics: An Analysis of Developments from 1884–1906*, Somaiya Publications, 1970.